Aunty Marmalade

Ruth Young

To Izzy,

It was lovely to meet you.

Best wishes,

Ruth Young
2010.

Eloquent Books

Copyright © 2009

Eloquent Books
An imprint of Strategic Book Group
P.O. Box 333
Durham CT 06422
www.StrategicBookGroup.com

ISBN: 978-1-60693-893-5, 1-60693-893-2

Printed in the United States of America

To Charles, Lottie and Olivia, as always.

It was my first night in a strange bed. I could imagine what it must be like to sleep in custard because this bed was almost too soft and cosy. The wind whispered through the gaps in the windows making the curtains twitch. The house was still and quiet but I could hear the waves rippling on the beach below. I felt myself drifting off to sleep. The sea air made me sleepy. It was then that I heard a soft thud above me coming from the attic. My eyes opened and I felt my heart thump. I dared not breathe. I held my breath. There it was again. A soft thud. Followed by another and another. They were getting louder and nearer. Then they stopped. I strained my ears and lay completely still. I half expected something or someone to fall through the ceiling and land on the bedroom floor but nothing happened. All I could hear was the sound of my breathing.

Aunty Marmalade

Gentle, gentle. Pretend you're not here.

Thud, thud this time getting quieter as they moved away from above my room until once again there was silence. I gulped a breath. I sat upright. A shiver went down my spine. I had a feeling someone or something was watching me...

Chapter1

I stood on the station platform and I wondered what to do next. I felt the cool sea air and smelt its saltiness. Overhead, seagulls screeched and dived at the fishing boats as they steamed towards the little harbour. The station was deserted. There was no guard like in the old films. I looked at the station name, panicking for a second that I was at the wrong station. But no, it was the right one; so where was Aunty Marmalade?

I came to Tarlton–on–Sea to stay with Aunty Marmalade while my parents went on a business trip to Australia. Aunty Marmalade was not her real name. It was Madeleine, my godmother, my mum's unmarried

Aunty Marmalade

older sister, and she had no children. She was almost identical to my mum and people often thought they were twins. But they were nothing alike in every other way. Aunty M was just one year older and much more fun. Nothing seemed to ever bother her. When I was little, I couldn't say her name but I could say 'marmalade' which I had on my toast. So I was the reason why everyone called her Aunty Marmalade.

Aunty Marmalade was famous in the family for her amazing hats with fruit and flowers sticking out of the tops and sides. She wore hats to try to control her red frizzy hair which bobbed about as she talked and even after she combed it, it still escaped and did exactly what she didn't want it to do. My hair was the same. She was really wacky and so unlike my mum. Mum always had her hair cut really short like a boy. Aunty M's was long and unruly. She loved breaking the rules and not conforming. I thought she was great, easy to be

8

with and great fun. The only problem was she didn't visit very often and we never visited her. Mum always said she was too busy. She blamed everything on working full time and *me*.

"It doesn't matter how many times I try to tidy your hair, it still does what it wants to," spat my mum as she dragged a comb through my tangles. "You get more like Aunty Marmalade every day."

My mum gave me strict instructions to follow for the journey and the stay because she never trusted me to do anything right. As mum said goodbye to me, she snapped, "Now Florence, when you arrive at the station Aunty Marmalade will be there to meet you."

"I don't really know her that well mum. What will I do if she doesn't want me for two weeks?"

"Don't be ridiculous. She doesn't mind looking after you. She's my sister for goodness sake. She owes me you know, big time, if only you knew, but that's another story. Anyway there was no one else to ask.

Now listen once more. She will be at the ...."

I had heard these instructions so many times. I
smiled and tried to look like I was listening but I knew
it all by heart.

"Have you remembered your book? Don't
forget to do your holiday diary and don't let her fill you
up with stodge. You look enough like her as it is."

"I won't. I'll tell her I'm not allowed."

"Good. There's no excuse nowadays to be
overweight."

"I've forgotten my book, Mum."

"Florence, how many times do you have to be
told? Now what are you going to do?"

"I could ask Aunty Marmalade to lend me a
book."

"You are supposed to be no trouble, Florence.
Just stay there and keep out of mischief and don't

bother Aunty Marmalade. She's not used to children.
She won't understand you like I do. You know that. I
give up with you. Here's your train. Try to do as I have
asked you for this once. Please."

With that she had turned around and stomped
away without even a smile, let alone a hug. *Why did I
always do everything wrong? Why didn't I just keep
quiet about forgetting my book? Why did my mum not
like me? Why was I such a nuisance to her?*

I had a sick feeling in my throat and I felt hot
and wished I hadn't put my fleece on under my anorak.
It seemed like a good idea when I packed my rucksack,
as it was too bulky to fit in to the space on top. Mum
told me I had to fit everything in the one bag as I
wouldn't be able to lift a suitcase. My rucksack wasn't
that big so I didn't have that much with me. I'd have to
ask Aunty Marmalade to wash stuff for me.

"Don't be a nuisance, Florence."

Aunty Marmalade

I won't be. But I will be smelly.

As all these thoughts and feelings made tears prickle my eyes, I heard a squeal of brakes and saw a cloud of dust just like the genii arriving in the pantomime at Christmas. As the dust settled, I could see an ancient vintage car with huge front lamps and a running board down the side. The door opened and out marched Aunty Marmalade, huffing and puffing towards me, wearing a huge floral tent dress and an old leather pilot's helmet and goggles.

Chapter 2

"Florence, honeybun, I'm sorry I'm late. There was a cow in the road and Farmer Peterson couldn't get it back in the field. I was stuck in the road for ages. Anyway no damage done and here we are. How are you? You have grown. I would hardly have recognised you. Mind you, it must be at least a year or two since I saw you last."

Without waiting for a reply, I felt myself being lifted off my feet and squeezed until I could hardly breathe, but when I did, I got the familiar smell of lavender that reminded me of her.

As she released me, I spluttered, "I'm fine and really pleased to see you. At first I thought I'd got off at

13

the wrong station and mum would go ballistic when she found out."

"Huh, well you know Florence if you had, we wouldn't have told her. What she doesn't know won't worry her, that's my way."

I looked at Aunty M's smiling rosy face and I felt better, not so worried.

"How are you Aunty M?"

"Fine just '*spondoolucks*' as always, my dear."

With that, she picked up my rucksack and threw it on the back seat of the car next to Biggles; her yellow Labrador. He was also wearing a helmet and goggles like Aunty M. The seat all around him was covered in dog hairs and he was panting and drooling and a pool of slobber built up beside him. He was gorgeous. I had heard of Biggles many times had but never met him. Mum never let him come with Aunty M when she visited us.

14

"And that smelly, flea-bitten old mutt she lives with, I wouldn't let it past the front door," my mum said.

As I watched Aunty M tickle his nose with such kindness and fondness, I now realised why we had not had a visit from her for quite some time.

I got into the front seat and stretched back and stroked Biggles' head and he licked my hand and then sneezed and I felt wet all over my fingers, better wash my hands before I eat anything.

Don't be a nuisance. Keep out of the way. Do as you're told Florence.

I could see mum's steely grey eyes piercing through me, giving me a sense of dread.

Chapter 3

We sped along the country lanes and headed out

towards the sea on the coast road. High, on what looked

like the edge of the cliff, was a very large white house.

"There's Apple Jack's Cottage," said Aunty M

pointing to the house with her stubby finger.

Apple Jack's Cottage was old, white, and

beautiful. It had five windows on the first floor and four

on the ground floor with a huge dark blue front door in

the middle with an enormous knocker in the centre.

There were at least seven or eight chimneys sticking out

of the roof and what looked like up the side. It was in

the middle of a large garden which ended abruptly at the edge of the cliff.

"We'll have tea and cake first and then I'll take you up to your room and you can unpack," said Aunty M, "You must be tired after your journey, but first things first. I'll put the kettle on."

The kitchen was big and cluttered; it was nothing like ours at home which always smelled of bleach and disinfectant. Here, there were pots and pans hanging from the ceiling, jars of home made jams and pickles on shelves that sloped up and down, and I wondered how nothing fell off the end. There were dozens of ancient cookery books, all dog eared and well- read and a delicious smell of chocolate, pizza, and sausages all rolled into one.

Aunty M put cups and saucers and matching plates on the table and those small silver pastry forks that people had years ago and I had seen in a Victorian museum on a school trip. Then, she cut two enormous wedges of the tallest chocolate cream cake I had ever seen, put it on the plates, and drizzled runny chocolate sauce all over the top. She pushed one of the plates towards me.

"Tuck in," she sniggered with a naughty giggle.

I put a forkful in my mouth. I got a funny sensation in the back of my throat and my mouth filled with saliva. It was delicious and chocolaty. I had never tasted anything like this before. It dissolved in my mouth and I swallowed. I shoved another forkful in my mouth.

"Mum wouldn't approve of this cake," I said and realised that at home, I'd get another telling off for speaking with my mouth full.

"Your Mum has gone very healthy. She used to tuck into chocolate cake when we were kids, you know. It's a shame she became so serious. She used to have a really infectious giggle years ago. We were always

getting into scrapes together. I have no intention of ever

growing up, let alone becoming serious."

"Really? I don't want to grow up either." I

looked across the table at Aunty M who now had

chocolate coated lips which she then wiped with the

back of her hand. And as I had finished too, I did the

same.

Chapter 4

I followed Aunty M up the central staircase. We turned right at the top and walked to the far end of the long landing and she opened the last door. Inside, the room was all white with a blue border just below the ceiling. As I looked more closely, I could see the border was a line of fish, mermaids, and all sorts of sea creatures all intertwined. This pattern was on the bedcover, curtains, and painted on the wardrobe and the chest of drawers. In front of the window was a dressing table with curtains around the drawers. On top was a posy of wild flowers in a little blue pot and a brush, comb, and mirror with blue flowers embroidered on

20

them. The window was open and I could hear the waves crashing on the beach below and the calls of the seagulls as they fished in the breakers.

In the corner of the room were some shelves that went right up to the ceiling. Each shelf had a few books, seaside mementoes, and peculiar looking wooden objects on it. As I looked more closely I realised the shelves got narrower as they went up.

"This was your mum's room when we were little," said Aunty M as she grabbed the pillows on the bed and puffed them up turning them over and over until they were so high that my head would never reach them tonight. It seemed strange looking around the room now knowing that it had been mum's room. The room was pretty and girlie. Our house was so *white* and not fussy at all with only the bare minimum of furniture.

Aunty Marmalade

"Mum doesn't talk about when she was little. She's always so busy at work so I've found it easier not to bother her unless I really have to," I commented as I stood on tip-toes to look at the view from the window.

"That's the trouble today. Everyone is so busy and no one has time to talk anymore. I had guessed that things may not be too easy for you at home. Your mum is granny-like, very bossy with a very sharp temper."

"It's Ok really but I'll be glad to go to boarding school in September because she won't have me to worry about. I won't feel so bad then." I didn't want to sound too disloyal, but I meant what I said.

"That's the ticket and I hope that will mean that you'll come and stay whenever you can in the holidays and we can eat everything that's bad for us and stay up late and read *Hello* and *OK* Magazine and we won't tell a soul because nobody needs to know."

I said that sounded great.

Chapter 5

The rest of the day, we spent walking Biggles along the beach to the rocks at the end of the cove.

"So how is school these days?"

"It's Ok but I'll be glad to leave. I'm the only one going to St Maur's in my class so I won't know anyone."

"It will be a fresh start then for you. That's never a bad thing. I understand from mum that you have done really well to get a place at St Maur's."

"I am pleased to get a place. I'm going to really try hard there to please mum."

Aunty Marmalade

That evening after dinner, Aunty Marmalade went to finish her painting in her studio. She painted pictures of the sea's countryside which she then sold in a local gallery. Her studio and bedroom was at the far end of the long landing at the opposite end from me. I had seen one of her pictures hanging along the landing. I wasn't sure whether I liked it or not because all the colours were bright and not like the real thing at all. It was a landscape and the odd thing too was the trees had pineapples and bananas growing on them. I'd never seen fruit like that growing in England, but I didn't say anything of course, only that I liked them.

I lay on my bed listening to my ipod and flicking through my *Mizz* magazine. There was a really good bit about what to wear in the summer and a free eye shadow and brush. Aunty M said that I could try it out in the morning. It was great to be treated a bit grown up. She said there was no reason why I couldn't keep it on all day.

That night, I woke with a start. I wasn't sure at first what had woken me up. The wind was howling through the window as the weather had gotten worse since this afternoon. I heard something crack and what sounded like a whisper. I couldn't tell what was said. I strained my ears, annoyed that the wind was gusting now and making it hard to hear clearly. Then as the wind subsided, I definitely heard someone say,

"Florence."

It was then I heard steps. I couldn't tell whether they were coming from the landing or above me in the attic. *It must be Aunty Marmalade.* I got up and walked to the door and slowly, it creaked open. Silence. There was no noise on the landing. Aunty Marmalade was certainly nowhere to be seen. It couldn't be her. She would have called again if she wanted me, but why would she want me anyway? I glanced at the digital

clock. The red numbers glowed 1:30. Suddenly scared,

I ran back to bed and lay there listening, wanting to

hear and yet not wanting to hear. I tried to convince

myself that it was just the wind playing tricks on my

mind. Perhaps I had dreamed it. I know dreams can feel

very real. I know sometimes you're asleep but you

think you're awake. But I knew this time, I was awake

and I had heard my name whispered. I closed my eyes

and counted sheep. By the time I got to fifty-eight, my

eyes felt heavy. My room was silent once more but I

felt unnerved. I had a real feeling that someone was

trying to contact me.

Chapter 6

The next morning after breakfast, I went back upstairs to my room. I heard a little tap on the door. The door nudged open and in came Aunty M. I unplugged my ipod from my ears and fluttered my eyelids showing off the eye shadow.

"Very glam I must say,' said Aunty M fluttering back."

"What do you think? Do I look daft or does it suit me?"

"I think you look lovely. The colour brings out the colour of your eyes and makes them look bigger. Now, I need to paint again today. I have to finish off

27

two paintings I'm exhibiting at the Annual Arts and Crafts Show at the weekend."

"Ok, Aunty M. I must write up my diary or mum will kill me. I have to do it every day and I didn't do it yesterday."

"So you're busy too. That's good. Now I really must get on. See you later. We'll have coffee and some chocolate chip cookies at eleven. I'll call you."

"Yum. Can I have coffee too?" I asked.

"Absolutely. You have to have coffee to bring out the flavour of the cookies!"

When Aunty M had left, I plugged back into my iPod and lay on my bed. I couldn't face writing my diary but I decided it was best to get it over and done with. I put my diary and furry rabbit pencil case on the bottom shelf in the corner of the room, and went back to the bed to lie down. Nick Delenti was singing his latest track in my ears and I found I couldn't help

28

wriggling my toes in time to the music. I looked up at the ceiling. It bowed down in several places. There were lots of cracks like long wrinkles across it too. The cottage must be really old. Then as I looked towards the corner where the shelves were, I noticed a square cut into the ceiling above the top shelf.

I became curious. What could it be? Why would anyone cut the ceiling? I walked over to the shelves. The bottom step was very wide and they got narrower as they went up. I realised they were a hidden stairway that led up to a hatch, which must open up to the attic.

This was exciting. A secret stairway. I wonder if mum knew about it. Yes, she must have known. Well, this was her room after all. Without thinking and without asking if I could, I made a space on the shelves as I started to climb up. There were a few dusty pots and a vase of dried flowers but they were old and faded and they looked rather sad. There were also some old books and a pile of old comics from when mum was little. They looked old fashioned and well-read. When I had cleared a space up the shelves, I stood back and looked.

I climbed up. It wasn't easy as there were no banisters, then when I got to the top, I could see a brass ring which had been painted white like the ceiling, on the hatch. I grabbed the ring, pulled and down came a panel. I was showered with dust but I could see up inside the attic. I held on to the edge of the hole, with my legs dangling down. Then I swung my legs to give me more momentum and with all my strength, I hauled myself up.

I glanced around. The attic was full of dusty, cobwebby book shelves, trunks that looked like pirates once owned them and racks of dressing up clothes. My heart jolted as I caught sight of what looked like a huge headless doll in the corner but as my eyes got used to the dim light, I saw it was one of those dummies dress

makers use. At the far end of the attic was a huge

arched window. It had a stained glass pattern at the top

and was very dirty and so let in very little light. The

attic was gloomy and the shadows that the light made

were odd and sort of spooky. I didn't feel scared just

excited really. There must be all sorts of treasures and

secrets and stuff from years ago up here. I thought back

to my project on the Victorians that I must get down to.

Maybe I'd find pieces of Victorian junk that I could

take to school. I couldn't wait to start exploring.

It was then that I remembered the noises I had

heard coming from up here. A cold sensation trickled

down my spine. I glanced around suddenly feeling that

there was something behind me. I turned slowly around.

Nothing. "Stop being silly," I said out loud to myself.

"The wind and old houses are always spooky and

creaky and make scary noises. Well, they always do in scary books and films."

I walked down towards the window and in front of it was a red, squashy, well used sofa. I guessed that's where Aunty M and my mum would have sat and read in the peace and quiet when they were little. There were two deep dents one either side of it.

"That's where they must have sat," I found myself saying aloud.

I ran my fingers across the velvety pile. The whole, battered sofa had lost its springs but there was a bit of stuffing left to make it comfortable. I'd come up and write my diary later.

By the side of the sofa was an old wooden box. It was inlaid with gold leafy patterns across the top and a key hole on the side. I tried to lift the lid but it was locked.

"I wonder where the key is?" I heard myself say aloud again. *I really must stop talking to myself.*

I pulled the box towards me. It was really heavy and it scraped across the floor. Behind the box I noticed a little door cut in the wall. It had a rusty old key in the lock and a piece of faded ribbon was knotted around the end. What was that door doing there? I tried to turn the key but it wouldn't budge. I pushed the door in a bit and tried again. It reluctantly turned, hurting my fingers, but I hoped it would be worth it. The door creaked towards me. Instantly, there was a musty smell and a breath of cold air. As my eyes got used to the darkness, I could see a large black box and what looked like a photo album. I was intrigued. *Who would want to hide a box and a photo album? And what was I going to find?*

Chapter 7

I pulled out the box which was tied up with a
very dirty, faded piece of white ribbon. It had a label on
top which said, 'Wedding Dress 1996.' I dragged out
the photo album and flicked through the photos. There
were brown, black and white and coloured photos. Why
would anyone want to hide these things? I looked at the
box. I untied the ribbon and pulled it from around it; I
lifted the lid and shook it gently. The bottom of the box
thumped onto the floor. Inside there was a fold of black
tissue paper. I gently parted the tissue, and inside I saw
a little satin bag and what looked like a wedding dress.
The dress was made of soft, shiny white material which

was now quite yellowed. I lifted the dress out held it up to me and gazed into an old, cracked mirror which was in front of one of the book shelves. The gown was beautiful. Layers of petticoats puffed out the skirt and tiny covered buttons stretched down the back while rows and rows of tiny pearls adorned the front and the back. Unfortunately, the cupboard was so cold and damp that a musty smell permeated the room. I went back to the box and took out the satin bag. Inside was a coronet of waxy flowers with a gauzy veil attached to it; I placed it carefully on my head. I went back to the mirror. I stared at myself. A ghostly figure stared back at me. Suddenly I lost my nerve.

"What are you doing?" I said aloud, realizing I had unearthed something private; something that was nothing to do with me. I touched someone's secret world. "How would you feel?" I asked myself.

Aunty Marmalade

It was then that I thought I heard a breathy voice say, "Put it back. Put it back."

Looking all around me I could see no-one. It must be the wind again. I realised how spooky it was up here. Could the wind be sending me messages? I'd been watching too many cartoons about creepy mansions. Then I realised how excited I had become. This was better than staying with a child minder any day. I was going to have plenty to tell Eloise, my best friend at school, after the holidays. Plenty in fact.

But I felt that I may have disturbed something. My flesh started to creep. It just felt wrong. I felt awful at what I had done. I folded the dress and quickly put it back in the box along with the coronet and slammed down the lid. I pulled the ribbon and tied it back round the box. I pushed it back into the cupboard. Whoever had worn the dress had had something happen to them of that I felt sure. Would the album help me to find out?

My curiosity was charged. I knew I shouldn't look inside but I lifted the green leather cover of the album.

It was then that my mobile phone rang. I climbed backwards down the shelves and grabbed my phone.

"Hello, who's there, its Florence?"

Silence. Nothing Then from faraway a breathless whisper answered me, "Florence, Florence, Florence."

Then the line went dead.

Chapter 8

Whoever it was knew my name. Strangely my phone read, 'no-caller,' so I had no idea who it could have been. I decided to find Aunty M. It's not normal to keep hearing things is it? No, I must be losing my marbles. I ran to find her.

"Hello Aunty M, am I interrupting you?"

"No not at all dear. Are you Ok? Fancy that coffee now? I'm desperate."

"Yes, me too. I'll go and put the kettle on."

I walked down to kitchen and felt safer there. My imagination was running wild. I decided not to tell Aunty M about finding the attic. I wanted time to explore more and if she knew she might stop me. I also decided not to say anything about the noises. She'd think I was attention seeking or something. I knew I must not be a nuisance. Probably just better to pull myself together and stop being silly.

My curiosity was getting the better of me. Later, I went back up to the attic. The photo album turned out to be full of old photos of Aunty M and my mum when they were little. There were also photos of my mum on the beach or playing in the garden with a dog very similar to Biggles. That must have been Ranger. I had heard my granny talking about him. There were lots of photos of people I did not recognise and I guessed they must be friends of the family. Then, towards the end of the album, there were some wedding photos. The man in the first photo was very tall and dark. I'd never seen him before and yet somehow he looked familiar and I couldn't think why. I was just about to turn over to the next page, when I heard Biggles' nails scraping on the wooden floor of my room. I had to get down because Biggles meant that Aunty M must be around. The last thing I wanted was for her to find me in the attic. There was a lot more investigating to do up there. I had just pulled the hatch down and got down the steps when Aunty M appeared in the doorway.

"There you are Biggles, come on let's go walkies. Are you coming too Florence? Darling, I do think you ought to make your bed in the morning. There's nothing worse than getting into an unmade bed. Very uncomfortable."

Feeling a bit shaken by the close shave, I looked at the room in disbelief. I had to think quickly.

My bed, which I had made that morning, was completely messed up. The duvet was on the floor, the pillows trampled on and stuffed under the bed. Not only that, but the curtains were drawn and every drawer and the wardrobe doors, were open. It looked like I had been burgled. I had only been in the attic about half an hour. I walked through my room before I went up and my room was tidy. All this happened while I was up there. But what was more to the point, whoever had done this, did it, silently just under me, to get me into trouble.

"Aunty M, I am so sorry. I just forgot to make my bed and tidy up earlier. I couldn't find my iPod and I became frantic because mum would murder me if I lost it. I won't let it happen again. Mum would go mad if I did this at home."

"All forgotten darling. My mum, your granny, used to tell me off constantly for being untidy so I know what it's like! I just want you to have a good night's sleep and you can't do that in an untidy bed. Let's go."

Aunty Marmalade

We walked on the beach and the sea air cleared my head. *I didn't remember untidying my bed. I knew I had not. I can't have forgotten to tidy my room. I always make my bed and close drawers because if I don't my Mum goes off on one of her rants and I avoid those at all costs. Perhaps the sea air is fuddling my head,* I thought.

That night as I lay in bed, I tried to piece everything together. The phone call, the untidy room, the thuds upstairs and the voices "What's going on?" I whispered to myself. Then I suddenly thought. *Someone is trying to contact me but who?*

Chapter 9

The following day it rained quite heavily. Aunty M was busy in her studio so I decided to go up to the attic to finish looking at the album. Everything looked the same up there. I had a look at the rack of dressing up clothes and there were some gorgeous silk dresses and amazing matching hats. There were fur stoles with the foxes head and feet still attached and the weirdest shoes with round toes and buttons.

"These must be great granny's and granny's dresses when they were young." I said aloud to myself.

It was comforting to hear my voice. Because I am an only child, I do tend to talk to myself.

Aunty Marmalade

Unfortunately, once at school I'd gone to the loo and thought I was alone. I chatted to myself and Felicity, one of the 'cool gang', came in and heard me. She called me, "Dingbat" and told everyone so then everyone called me that. They won't call me that at my new school.

I picked up the album and carried it to the sofa and made myself comfortable. I turned back to the wedding photos. I turned over to the next page. There was the wedding group a huge crowd of small faces stared back at me. There was the man I'd seen in the photo before. He was the groom. Then I recognised the dress. The bride was wearing the wedding dress and the coronet and veil in the box.

That's who wore the dress, I thought to myself. As I looked more carefully I realised that the woman in the wedding dress looked like mum. The picture was so small but it was her. It was taken ages ago; eleven years ago, in 1996 and she would have looked different then. Then I realised what I had found. My mum married someone else before my dad. Why had she never told me? I looked more carefully at the groom but the picture was too small. I flicked back to the bigger picture and stared at the face. I didn't know him but he definitely looked like someone I knew. *Who was it?* I thought about everyone that came to our house. No I'd never seen him and yet he looked so familiar. He had black hair and blue eyes, and a gap between his two front teeth. I have blue eyes and a gap between my teeth too. I turned over a couple of pages. There were more wedding pictures. The bride and this man smiling and happy. I looked along the line of guests. There was granny and granpy and Aunty M. I turned over to the next page. Baby pictures. Two dear little babies. Twin babies. They were dressed the same and looked the same. As I looked at the photo, I shivered. I was one of the babies. I had photos like this one at home taken

when I was little but I was always alone. Well I would

be because I was an only child. But here were two

identical babies. *Who was the other baby? And why did*

she look the same as me?

Chapter 10

I wandered down to the kitchen. How could I ask Aunty M why I was in the photo and who was the other baby? If I asked, I would have to tell what I had been doing in the attic. The babies looked just the same as me, when I was a baby. Identical in fact. I had unearthed so many secrets. Secrets that I needed answers to, but who could I ask? These were the sort of questions I needed to ask mum. Suddenly I had a strange feeling in my tummy. Perhaps the reason the man in the photo looked familiar was that I looked a little like him. The hair was different, but his eyes and the gap between his front teeth were like mine. I couldn't explain why but somehow I felt like I knew

this man, that he was somehow connected with me.

Then I had a shocking thought. Perhaps the man in the

photo was my father. But where was he now? What

happened to him? Why was mum not still married to

him? My life was somehow not going to be the same.

Who am I? I was jolted out of my daydream by the

phone ringing.

"Hello. Mum? Gosh how are you?" I spluttered

down the phone. She was the last person I thought

would phone.

"Hello, it's us. We're in Sydney. Just thought

we'd phone to find out how everything is?"

Huh. What did she think? I had three questions

to ask her just to start with. Who did you marry before

dad, who is my father and why are there two babies that

look like me? But it's not easy to ask when she was ten

thousand miles away.

"We are fine. I'm having a lovely time. Aunty M and I are getting on really well."

"I hope you're behaving yourself. I don't want to hear you've been trouble Florence, if this works well, I'm sure Aunty M will have you again and it sounds like you like it there."

"Yes I do, and I do want to stay again and I am being good."

"Good. Well, better say goodbye. See you when we get back."

"How's dad?" But all I heard was the click and the dial tone.

I turned to see Aunty M coming into the kitchen. Her hair was tied up in a floral scarf; tied up in the front like the ladies in the old black and white films in the war.

"That was mum on the phone," I said with a lump in my throat. I stared at the shelf of jams and pickles and tried to pretend I was interested in them even though I wasn't. I didn't want Aunty M to realise I was so disappointed that mum couldn't even think of anything to say to me, like she missed me.

"Oh, how are they?" she asked and I could feel her eyes penetrating through my clothes into my back willing me to turn around.

"Mum didn't say much about what they are doing. She just wanted to remind me to be good," I replied feeling a terrible sadness overwhelm me.

"Well at least she phoned sweetcake. She doesn't mean to be so sharp. I think she just doesn't *think.* "

"Would it be Ok if I took Biggles for a walk along the beach?" I asked wiping my runny nose on the back of my hand.

"That would be such a help Florence. I must get this picture finished and it would mean I could carry on."

"Walkies Biggles, come on."

Biggles and I walked to the end of the garden. He ran ahead of me down the wooden steps to the sand. As I walked along, I tried to clear my head but I couldn't. My life was not the same at all any more. It looked like my dad was not my dad and who was the other baby in the photo?

It was only drizzling now and Biggles jumped in and out of the waves. I threw a stick in for him and he charged in for it, but as he dived in, a wave caught him and tossed him under. He bobbed up to the surface only to be knocked down again. He started paddling furiously but made little progress towards the beach. I realised he was struggling and that I had to help him and with that, I found myself plunging into the waves.

51

Aunty Marmalade

The water was icy cold and the waves bigger than I thought, but it did not matter; I had to save Biggles. I trod water but the sea heaved me up and tossed me down. As I bobbed up I saw a flash of yellow. Biggles was swimming towards me rising and falling on the swell. As the next wave rose and fell, I reached for his collar but the wave he was on went back out again. Then a wave caught me and tossed me under. I didn't know whether I was up or down. Then I bobbed up and shouted,"Biggles, swim, swim," I screeched but the wind caught my voice and carried it away. I could feel myself being dragged further and further out.

I started to cry out his name again and again. It was hopeless. I felt exhausted and desperate. We were both going to drown. My body almost started to relax as I realised there was nothing I could do to save Biggles or myself.

My fleece suddenly tugged and I felt like I was being strangled. I fell back on the sand. Next to me was Biggles, panting, sneezing and coughing.

"Biggles, you're Ok. Thank God." I flung my arms around his neck.

I looked around for whoever it was that had helped us. There was no-one there. Who saved me? A chill ran through me then an enormous sense of relief and thanks. I had had a close shave, and one I never wanted to repeat. But a nagging thought was in my mind that someone helped us but there was no-one on the beach but Biggles and me.

"Come on Biggles. Let's go home."

Together, we walked slowly back. What would Aunty M say? I knew I'd done the wrong thing in trying to rescue him. I just didn't think. If anything had happened to him, I'd never forgive myself but I realised, I too, had been in danger and what's more, I was soaking wet.

I stuffed my clothes into the washing machine hoping Aunty M wouldn't notice my wet clothes; harm had been done and the last thing I wanted was for Aunty M to have to get cross with me. Up in my room, I quickly changed and it was then I noticed that the padlock on my diary had been opened.

Someone read about my secret thoughts. But who?

Chapter 11

"Aunty M? Is Apple Jack's Cottage always so creaky and groany?"

"Yes darling. It's because it's so old, about four hundred years old. The wind whistles through the windows and the floorboards bend and bow. Sometimes I think I'm not the only one living here. I find it quite comforting really. I love this old house. As you know, I've lived here most of my life."

"Yes, mum told me. Have you ever wanted to be married?"

"Yes, I did and I did fall in love once."

"What was he like?"

Aunty Marmalade

"He was tall and very handsome with a mop of thick black hair. He lived just down the coast road, so I'd known him all my life. We had always been friends and everyone just knew we would marry one day. But things didn't work out as I planned they would."

As I looked at Aunty M I could see her eyes were shiny with tears.

"Aunty M, I'm sorry I've distressed you. I didn't mean to." I gently placed my arms around her neck and her arms went around me.

"What a pair we are. Let's have a cup of tea."

As I sipped my tea, Aunty M looked at me, smiled and asked, "Been swimming recently Flo?"

"I've been meaning to tell you. Biggles got swept out to sea and I sort of went in to rescue him."

"Just promise me one thing darling. You won't do that again."

I promised.

Chapter 12

The following day I walked to the shops to buy my *Girl Talk* magazine and buy a pint of milk so Aunty M could make some custard to have with the apple pie she made that morning. It was a lovely day and I felt quite cheerful, but my mind was full of unanswered questions. I felt my life was turning upside down. I wanted to ask Aunty M to answer my questions but it all seemed too personal. It was awful to see her look so desolate when I asked her about being married. She might not even know what had happened all those years ago and even if she did, she might not want to tell me or get involved.

Aunty Marmalade

I got my comic and the milk and as I walked out of the shop, I turned left to walk home. As I continued on my way, I looked in the dress shop window because they always had lovely beads and stuff and I saw a gorgeous hair band. It had little beads and seashells on it. I looked for the price but the label was the wrong way up. I decided to go in and ask how much it was. A bell rang as I went in.

"Can I help you?" asked the lady behind the counter.

The hair band was quite cheap and the lady gave it to me to have a closer look. As I took it, I held it up to the light and as I did, I noticed someone on the other side of the road. For a second, I thought I could just see my reflection in the glass. She had long ginger hair just like mine. It was long and loose. She had her back to me so I couldn't see her face. Then as I stared, she slowly turned to face me. To my horror, I was looking at myself. I blinked and when I blinked, she wasn't

there. I was sure I had seen someone identical to myself

but who was she?

"I'm sorry," I spluttered to the lady I quickly

handed the hair band back to her and ran out of the

shop. I stared up and down the road. Nothing. No-one

even remotely like me was walking about. Think.

Think. It must have been my reflection after all but the

clothes weren't the same. I was wearing jeans,

converses and a white tee shirt with a green cardigan.

The girl was wearing a white dress and white plimsolls.

It could have been a girl, my age that looked similar to

me. Lots of girls have red hair. That must be it. You're

not going mad. There is always an explanation for

things like this. I heard dad say it a hundred times when

magicians were on the TV. He would even go on to

explain how the trick was done. Apparently, he'd had a

magic set when he was a little boy so he felt he was a
bit of an expert.

I walked back to Apple Jack's Cottage. My list
of unusual happenings was increasing day by day. My
best friend, Eloise wouldn't believe a word of all of
this. Not surprising really because I didn't believe it
myself.

That afternoon, I went back up to the attic.
Aunty M was busy painting and I knew I had to amuse
myself. I was used to that. I decided to try on one of the
dresses and hats on the clothes rack. I pulled the dress
over my head. It was far too long and big. I put on some
matching shoes and hat and stared at myself in the
mirror. I looked really funny and old fashioned. I
trotted down to the sofa in the high heels. I couldn't
imagine ever being able to walk in shoes like this. They
were so uncomfortable.

I opened a drawer in the old wooden bureau just to see what was in there. I found a tiny blue leather ring box and lifted the lid. Inside was the most beautiful engagement ring-- a blue stone in the middle with diamonds surrounding it. Perhaps it was Aunty M's. I glanced into the drawer again. There was a pile of letters tied up in a pink bow. Love letters. How romantic was that. She kept her letters from the man she loved and the ring too.

As I put the ring back, I noticed a long box. I took it out and took the lid off. Once again, like the wedding dress box, it was lined with black tissue paper. I carefully separated the tissue and found two baby dresses the sort you see at a christening. They were identical and long. They had ribbons and lace on them and each dress had a matching bonnet, the sort you see on Victorian dolls with ribbon ties. I wondered if these beautiful dresses belonged to the twins in the photo.

Aunty Marmalade

That meant if I was one of the twins, I had worn one of these dresses.

"I'm so confused," I said aloud. "What happened to the other twin? Where is she now? Why was I never told? I must have a sister, a twin sister. Why is it such a secret?"

Desperation filled me. Then I thought, perhaps it isn't me in the photo after all and I just look like the baby in the photo. Babies do sort of look the same. That must be it. Yeah, I just look like that baby. Dad would have told me even if mum wouldn't. He's always so honest that he's bound to have told me. Even though he treats me like a baby most of the time, he'd never keep something like this from me. Why would he? No reason I could think of. Why do grown ups have so many secrets?

I took off the clothes and went to find Aunty M. She had finished painting and was making the custard.

There was a gorgeous smell of apples and custard and chicken.

"Hi. Yummy I'm starving Aunty M. You're the best cook ever."

"I hardly think so sweetie pie, but I do enjoy cooking and it's lovely to cook for someone else. Usually I just cook for myself."

That night my room was full of moonlight. It was a clear night and the inky black sky was dotted with millions of sparkling stars. Eerie shadows danced around my room as the cool night breeze, as always, tickled my curtains. Above me in the attic, a drawer shut so violently that my bed vibrated. I had definitely heard the noise that time. I did not imagine it; I knew I hadn't. I pulled the covers up under my eyes and waited breathless for the next noise but there was nothing. I had to find out. I had to know what was going on in the attic. I climbed the steps. I pulled the ring in the hatch.

Aunty Marmalade

The hatch swung down. I stuck my head up through the hole. Then everything went black.

Chapter 13

"Oh my God, Florence what happened? Are you alright?"

I was lying on the bedroom floor. My head hurt and so did my back.

"I'm not sure. I must have fallen out of bed."

'Can you move your legs?'

I could; although I felt stiff and very shaken. Aunty Marmalade helped me up.

"I heard a terrible crash Florence. If I hadn't you could have been here all night."

"I've fallen out of bed before Aunty M. Mum says my bed looks like I've been wrestling gorillas. She goes mad with me. She says I ought to try to lie still but you can't help what you do when you're asleep can you?"

"Don't worry about mum, for goodness sake. As long as you are alright and there is no damage to you; she need never know. Now back to bed and we'll see how you are in the morning."

"Yes, I'm fine. Just a bit shaky. Aunty M?"

"Yes, my darling?"

"Do you ever hear funny noises?"

"What sort of noises, darling?" asked Aunty M as she plumped up the feathers in my duvet.

"Sort of thumps and bumps and moans. That sort of thing."

"Of course. It's the wind. It makes the most awful noises. Even I get spooked sometimes."

"Do you?"

"Yes I do. I'm a real ninny aren't I?"

"No you're not. You're the best, Aunty M. See you in the morning."

As Aunty M walked out, I tried to think back to when I got to the hatch. As it fell down it must have knocked me. Yeah, it was so dark that must be it. I lost my footing and fell back. I was lucky I didn't break anything or worse. I looked towards the hatch. It was closed. I couldn't have closed it so someone must have. Aunty M would have seen the open hatch if it was open. Then she would have known that I was going up to the attic. As I drifted off to sleep I heard, very faintly, but definitely, the sound of someone calling out my name.

Chapter14

The following morning I was certainly bruised, but apart from that, there was no other permanent damage. Aunty M was busy packing her two pictures ready for the Arts and Crafts Show.

"We'll have to go to the Village Hall later to hang these up ready for the exhibition tomorrow. I do hope they sell. It's always exciting when you sell paintings."

"They are bound to be sold because they are so good," I said and I meant it. These two paintings were the best I had seen so far, not quite so colourful, more realistic.

"Let's hope you're right, darling."

Aunty M had a good place for her pictures just inside the entrance. I continued to look around at all the other stuff on show. There were lots of stupid pictures which were so badly painted I thought I could do better myself. Aunty M said a lot of what was on show was pretty dreadful, but that the exhibition gave lots of pleasure to lots of people and that was all that mattered. Some were so bad I could hardly imagine who would get pleasure from them. Some of them just gave me the giggles and I had to pretend I had a coughing fit so as not to get into trouble for being rude.

One of the last paintings on show was a small little oil painting of two girls. They were wearing identical clothes. Long white frilly dresses, bonnets and both were carrying parasols. It was a Victorian scene and quite well painted. As I looked more closely, I noticed a house in the background. It was just the same as Apple Jack's Cottage. The faces on the girls were not clear but they were the same height with long red hair.

"Aunty M there's a picture over here will you come and see?"

"Which picture is that, dear?"

I led her over to the painting.

"How extraordinary. That painting is of your great, great grandmother and her sister. It was up in the attic years ago and it must have got muddled up with the jumble I put together the last time I went up there. Mind you, that was quite a while ago. I wonder who is exhibiting it?"

Aunty M shuffled off to the organiser to try to find out.

"How very odd they said the painting is down as mine, but I didn't put it in the exhibition. There is no price on it so it won't be sold. I'm pleased about that it would be a shame to lose it out of the family. We can

70

take it home after the show ends. I think I better put it up on the wall to keep it safe from now on. I wonder who would have bought it and then given it back to me. I must say it's a very kind person. Wish I knew, I'd like to thank them."

"Yes," I agreed, "it is odd but sort of kind too."

Something was niggling at me. Perhaps the painting had been given back for a purpose to bring it sort of 'home.' It could have been 'stolen back.'

"Do you think we ought to take it now just in case there's been a mistake and it shouldn't be here?"

"I think you might be right Florence. It's in my name and it shouldn't be here anyway. I'll take it now."

Aunty M took down the painting put it in her basket and covered it with her cardigan.

Later that evening, the painting was hanging on a nail on the sitting room wall. The two little girls were back home, I thought. It was all mysterious how it came about. Funny the painting had been in the attic and because of that not missed. A picture of two little girls back together at home where they belong.

Later that evening, even though I was aching a bit from my bruises, I climbed the steps to the attic. I wanted to see if I could work out which drawer I heard slam the night before. I pulled myself up and what I saw shocked me.

The wedding dress was on the dummy with the coronet balanced on the top. The christening robes were laid across the top of the chest of drawers with the bonnets on top. Photos of my mother's first wedding were strewn around the floor. Photos of me and the other baby were there too, on the floor, but there was more. The baby photos were cut in half so the twins were separated. It was horrible. Who would do such a thing? I realised this was a sign; a sign to show that the twins had been separated. They were not together now or maybe not ever.

I thought about the painting. It had been retrieved from wherever it had been sold, to bring it back to where it belonged. Twins need to be together, back home together. That's why twins are so close. I heard that identical twins often think the same, talk the same and have the same thoughts. Well if I was a twin perhaps my twin was trying to reach me. Perhaps this was why all these strange things had happened to me since I came to Apple Jack's Cottage. I decided there and then to wait for the next sign and this time I would try to make contact. I sat down on the sofa and thought.

There were strange things happening here, sure there were, but sometimes at home, odd things happened too. I'd never thought about it before, but I never really felt lonely or alone. I had always put it down to being an 'only child.' When you are an 'only child' you have to sort of amuse yourself because there is no-one else there. In R.E lessons, my teacher talked about 'guardian angels' and I thought what a cool idea that would be to have one. You know, someone looking out for you, protecting you so you don't come to harm. As I sat there, I remembered the day I got out of dad's car and just walked into the road without checking first. A car shot pass just in front of me nearly knocking me down, but I missed it by a whisker. I always thought my 'guardian angel' saved me. Perhaps she had. Maybe she really did 'exist.'

The more I thought about it, the more I remembered other things that happened to me that I couldn't explain. I always felt like I was sharing my thoughts with someone else. That could be the reason I talked to myself. Yes, that could be it. I wasn't going dotty, I was sharing my thoughts and fears and good times with 'someone else'. Then there was the other

74

day in the sea. I felt my fleece tug and suddenly, I was on the beach.

I put the wedding dress and coronet back in the box. I placed the christening robes back too and gently closed the drawer. It must have been this drawer I heard slam last night. I put all the photos back in the album. I fitted the cut photos back together on the sticky paper. I shut the album with a bang.

"There you are. Everything sorted and back in its place. You can't scare me, whoever you are."

With that, I put my foot on the top step and climbed down into my room. I lay on my bed flicking through my *Girl Talk* magazine. There was a bit about working as an air stewardess. It was really interesting and I decided it would be something I would like to do.

"Florence come quickly. Granny is on the phone," called Aunty M from downstairs.

"Coming," I called back.

Aunty Marmalade

"Hello, Granny. Yes, I'm fine. Yes, I'm being good. No, I'm not missing mum and dad. Ok see you tomorrow. Bye."

"So we have visitors tomorrow Florence. Well that'll be nice won't it?"

"Yes, I haven't seen granny for ages," I replied.

I was a bit surprised. I knew granny didn't come to visit Aunty M too often because she always said it was too far to drive. I wondered what she wanted and what made her decide she had to come all this way.

Chapter 15

There was a beep on the horn and Aunty M and I knew granny had arrived. I ran out to meet her and she gave me one of her famous air kisses. She always smelled of the same flowery perfume and it was sort of comforting as it made me think of when I was little when granny looked after me quite often.

"Darling Florence. It is good to see you. You're looking very well I must say. Madeleine there you are. My goodness you too. You do look well. How are you?"

"We're both fine, spondoolucks really, thank you. Come in and have a cup of coffee you must be gasping after your drive," said Aunty M linking arms with granny.

After coffee, granny asked if she could see my room. She followed me upstairs and sat on the end of the bed.

"Are you alright dear? Is anything troubling you?"

"No I'm fine. I'm having a lovely time with Aunty M. She is so kind to me and never tells me off or anything. And we eat all the yummy stuff."

"Good, but are you sure everything is Ok?"

"Why do you ask?" I said puzzled.

"I phoned Madeleine the other evening and she mentioned that you had heard noises and she was worried about you. She doesn't understand too well about young people. She thought you might be too scared to talk to her about it."

"I have heard noises and stuff, but Aunty M told me it's only the wind and the old house creaking. Mum told me not to bother Aunty M and not to be a nuisance. I'm fine honestly. Mum and dad will be back soon anyway. But I love it here, really I do. Mum phoned the other day but she didn't say much. She just wanted to know whether I was being good."

"Mum doesn't mean to be so cold you know. She's just so busy and she's always put her career first. She should put you first we all know that, but that's the way she is and I don't think she'll ever change," said granny with an exasperated sigh.

"I know she won't change. I don't mind. I just want to do the right things for everyone. It will be better when I'm at boarding school."

"That's right. It will be better."

Aunty Marmalade

"Granny, have there ever been twins in our family apart from my great, great granny and her sister?"

"Twins? Goodness me. Um, no dearie, oh dear. Why do you ask?"

"No reason. I was just interested that's all when I saw the painting of the twins. It's amazing, isn't it seeing your ancestors. I even have the same hair as them," I replied. But as I did, I noticed the colour drain from granny's face and she started to fidget with her cardigan.

"You are a good girl Florence. I'm very proud of you."

Granny never spoke to me like this before. Her eyes were sparkly with tears and I couldn't understand why. But over the next few days, I did start to understand as the pieces of the jigsaw started to fit together.

Chapter 16

The next morning, Aunty M and I walked
Biggles along the beach. She stopped to talk to friends
and neighbours so Biggles and I walked on ahead to the
rocks at the far end. There were dinghies from the
sailing club bobbing about on the sea and the fishing
boats were coming back to the little harbour. Biggles
found a huge piece of drift wood which he dropped at
my feet so I could throw it into the sea for him.

"Ok Biggles, but only if you promise not to
swim out too far."

I threw the stick just a short way out, and he
found it and brought it back to me. We carried on with

the game until he got bored, and ran off to find a cuttlefish which he then devoured.

"Biggles you are revolting. Naughty boy." Just watching him made my stomach turn.

As I looked out to sea, I could see one of the dinghies suddenly dip and turn, and capsize. I wasn't sure if anyone saw what happened. I shouted to Aunty M and she came running towards me with one of her neighbours, Major Brunswick.

"Good Lord, they've capsized. We must get help and quick," shouted the Major.

"I'll run back to the house and phone," said Aunty M.

"I've got my phone with me, Aunty M." I dialled 999 and asked for help. Within a few minutes, there was a roaring sound and a lifeboat came speeding out of the harbour heading for the sinking dinghy. It was so exciting. I'd seen a rescue on the television but never in real life. The lifeboat was going so quickly dipping up and crashing down in the waves. Overhead, behind us came a roar. The noise was deafening as a helicopter flew just above our heads in the direction of the rescue scene. The helicopter hovered above the lifeboat whipping up spray and foam. We saw the hook go down with a rescuer dangling from it, and then the figure of a small person was pulled up held tightly by one of the rescue team. The helicopter came back towards us and flew passed on its way to the hospital in Madingly. The dingy bobbed back up the right way and was fixed onto a rope to be pulled along back by the lifeboat to the safety of the harbour.

Later that evening my mobile rang.

"Hello is that Florence?"

"Yes it is."

Aunty Marmalade

"Hi my name is Sam. Samantha Finn. I just wanted to say thank you for calling up the emergency services today. It was me that had to be rescued."

"Are you Ok?" I asked.

"Yes, just a bit shocked and embarrassed," came Sam's reply.

"I did nothing really. It was lucky I had my mobile with me."

"Yes, it was. But thanks for what you did. I owe you one. Where do you live?"

"In London, but I'm staying here with my godmother for a couple of weeks."

"I'll buy you a coke when I get out of hospital. I'll phone you again. Bye and thanks again," said Sam.

Great, I thought. Maybe a new friend. I hadn't met anyone since I'd been here and she might keep her promise and help me meet some others too. What an exciting day it'd been.

84

After supper, I washed up and decided to read while I was listening to my iPod. Aunty M was watching a programme on the TV about the Egyptians and I wasn't interested in it. I remembered I'd left last month's *Girl Talk* up in the attic and I wanted to finish reading it. So I climbed the steps pulled myself up and walked towards the sofa. As my eyes got used to the dim light, I saw someone sitting where I had been, reading my comic.

Chapter 17

A shudder ran down my spine. I stopped, unable to move. As my eyes desperately tried to focus on the figure, the light became so dim that the only way I could see better was to move closer to the sofa. I felt my foot move forward and as I did so the figure started to fade until it disappeared. My comic fluttered on to the sofa and I felt alone. I let my breath out and felt light-headed. I reached down, picked up my magazine and slumped down where the figure had been.

I rubbed my eyes. The light was dim up here. I must be seeing things. The wind was whistling through the gaps in the window. That must have been what moved the pages of my *Girl Talk*. That could be an explanation, I knew that.

"Is there anyone there?" I whispered, hoping I wouldn't get an answer and yet wishing in a strange way, I did.

But nothing happened. Whoever it was did not return. A terrifying feeling of loneliness came over me. The figure had stared at me. The eyes seem to stare through me but the most worrying part was those eyes were blue like mine. But they were lifeless. Pleading. Desperate. Sad. The more I thought about the figure, the more I realised that it looked like me. It was like looking at me in the mirror, and yet it wasn't me. Obviously, it can't be me. The figure was dressed all in white.

Suddenly I felt cold and I started to shiver. A feeling of absolute terror wafted over me like a wave and all I could think of doing was getting downstairs to my room and to safety. I backed towards the hatch

slowly, slowly. Sudden movements might make the

vision reappear. My heart was thumping in my chest.

My mouth was dry. I stumbled over a pile of shoes,

turned and as quickly as I could, I climbed down into

my room. Relieved that I had escaped; my heart

stopped pounding.

When odd things happen, there could always be

an explanation. Aunty M and granny made sense about

the noises I heard, but this time, I really did think I saw

a girl. I think I saw a ghost. The ghost looked like me

and may have wanted to make contact with me, but for

whatever reason this evening was not the right time.

Omigod. The realisation of what I was thinking was

really scary. I would have to wait until she felt she was

ready to trust me or get to know me better. Well, she

would need to know that I wouldn't scream and run or

rush off to tell Aunty M or granny. She needed to become my friend.

That night, I kept waking up thinking I could hear noises. At one stage I actually thought I saw a ghostly figure standing at the foot of my bed. I opened my eyes and rubbed them, but there was nothing there. There were no strange noises because the wind had dropped. Even the curtains didn't twitch.

In the morning, I jumped out of bed and tripped over my rucksack. I hadn't put it there. It had been moved from the bottom of the wardrobe. It must be a sign that she was trying to contact me again. I went down to the kitchen.

"Good morning Aunty M. How are you?"

"You're very chirpy today. Did you sleep well?"

"Yes I did," I lied not wanting Aunty M to become suspicious. "What are we doing today?"

Aunty Marmalade

"I must pop into town today to get some paints and paper. I need to get some serious painting done as four of my pictures have just been sold and I need to replace them. I wondered if you would like to visit Sam, the girl you helped rescue, at the hospital. We could 'kill two birds with one stone' as they say."

"I'd like to do that. I'd like to meet her. I think she's a bit older than me and it would be good to have someone to chat to so I don't have to keep bothering you," I replied.

"Florence, you could never be a bother to me you know that."

Aunty M put on her helmet and goggles. We got into the car and off we roared. Travelling in a car with the hood down is one way of getting your hair full of knots. My hair blew forwards, backwards, up and down and twisted itself around and around and by the time we got to town, I looked like one of those monsters in my

90

Latin text book. I could just imagine my Mum's face if she could see me now, and it wouldn't be pleasant for her or me. Now I knew why Aunty M wore the helmet.

After we bought her painting stuff, we set off to the hospital. It was a quaint building. It looked more like a pub than a hospital.

"Could you please let us know where we could find Sam Finn?" Aunty M asked the receptionist.

"Yes, she's in room number 7. Down the corridor and turn right," replied the receptionist. She smiled and we said our thank yous.

Sam was in the bed by the window. She turned around to look at us. She looked about my age with very short dark hair. She was covered in brown freckles and had a big wide smile.

"Hello, are you Sam?" I asked.

"Yes," came the reply, "Hi, there. Are you Florence?"

"Yes I am. This is my aunt. Aunty Marmalade."

"How do you do?"

"We were coming into town anyway and we thought you wouldn't mind if we popped in to see you," said Aunty M.

I handed Sam a huge bar of chocolate that I bought her. Aunty M said she would probably prefer it to grapes.

'No, it's great to meet you and it gives me a chance to say thanks for what you did for me. I've been sailing for ages but that day, the sea was quite rough and I just lost control of my dinghy. It was the first time it happened to me. I don't know what would have happened to me if you hadn't been there."

"When are you going home?" I asked.

"Tomorrow. I can't wait. The food in here is awful and there's nothing wrong with me. They just

wanted me to stay in for a few days 'under observation'
they said."

"Would you like to come over for tea when you
feel up to it?" I asked.

"Yes I would. Where do you live?" asked Sam.

"I'm staying at Apple Jack's Cottage."

"I only live about five minutes walk from you.
I'll come over on Thursday then about four?"

"Great," I said. 'See you then.'

"Thanks, Florence. Nice to meet you Aunty M."

"You too, Sam" Aunty M and I replied together.

We left and headed down the corridor.

"What a lovely girl she is," said Aunty M, "she
must live further down the coast road from us."

"Yes she is nice. How old do you think she is?"

"No older than you I would say maybe eleven or
twelve. You'll probably become firm friends. Then

whenever you come to stay you can catch up with each

other," suggested Aunty M.

"Yes," I replied enthusiastically. I was really

looking forward to Thursday. It seemed ages since I had

chatted to someone my age. Not that mattered. I'd had

plenty of excitement since I came to stay.

Chapter 18

Sam arrived at four bang on time.

"Hi come in. Let's have something to eat and drink and then I'll take you up to my room."

"Great. Wow what a tea," said Sam almost in disbelief.

Sam looked at the table in the kitchen. Aunty M had laid the table and is was full of lots of delicious treats.

"My aunt makes the best cakes ever. This one is lemon drizzle, this is chocolate with extra chocolate sauce and this is cream and jam sponge. There are scones if you prefer, or these are fruit and nut biscuits, or these are jumbo chocolate chips. There's tea, water or juice."

"Stop. Do you have this choice every day?" laughed Sam.

"Fraid so!" I responded. "Aunty M just loves baking and her cakes are really scrummy! What do you want to start with?"

"Can we have more than one?" asked Sam.

"Sure, she'd be hurt if we didn't tuck in and try everything," I said proudly.

"Ok, I'd love to try the chocolate one with the extra sauce. Can I have orange to drink?"

I cut two smallish slices and put them on plates and poured two glasses of juice.

I pushed a plate and glass to Sam and watched. Her reaction to the cake was just like mine when I had my first slice. She closed her eyes and said, "Wow it's amazing. I could eat the whole cake."

"Better not we've got two more to try after this."

We both laughed out loud and continued to chomp our way through the chocolate followed by the lemon and then the sponge.

"I'm stuffed," I said.

"Me too," groaned Sam, "My mum says, "I've had an adequate sufficiency," but to be honest, I am stuffed too."

"Let's go upstairs and you can see my room."

We went up the stairs followed by Biggles who was very excited that we had a visitor.

"Cool room. You've got a really soft bed."

"Yes, it's so soft. My one at home is hard like a board. My mum says it's good for my back but to be honest I think it's giving me backache." We both laughed.

Aunty Marmalade

"Parents can be a pain can't they. Always moaning and nagging. You just think you've got it right and they change the rules again," said Sam.

"My dad is Ok," I offered, "He's away a lot so he doesn't mind. I don't think he can be bothered. He has loads to do when he is at home so as long as I'm quiet and my reports are Ok, he doesn't say much."

"That's funny he sounds like my dad too. He's always away which means I only have my mum and my brother at home. I'm at boarding school are you?"

"No, but I'm going in September."

"Cool. Which one are you going to?" asked Sam with interest.

"St Maur's it's in…"

"Never. St Maur's in Deerling?"

"Yes."

"Well there's a coincidence as they say. That's where I go. I'm in Year 7 so I'll be going up to Year 8 in September."

"So I'll be the year behind you. When is your birthday?" I asked.

"I'll be twelve on 14th March."

"I'll be eleven on 28th March."

"How funny. We're nearly one year apart. I'll be able to look after you when you start. I'll ask if I can be your 'shadow.' We have a really good system for new girls. You'll love it there. I do. There's plenty to do, the work's not too bad and best of all, it's far away from parents. What more could you want?" said Sam smiling.

"I can't believe you go there. I've been a bit nervous about starting, but my mum works and I am a nuisance to her. I have to stay late every night at school until she can get me, so it will be better for her and me if I'm boarding. I want to make new friends too. There's a 'cool gang' in my class and I'm not part of it. I've been bullied and I'm too scared to tell my mum. It only makes things worse if you get the teachers involved."

"Poor you and you're right about the teachers. It won't happen at St Maur's. The teachers and the tutors make sure we are 'happy and thriving' to quote the Head, Mrs Postlethwaite. She's a dotty old bag but her heart's in the right place. Don't worry; you'll be fine and even better now you know me," said Sam smiling.

"Would you like to go up to the attic? There's all sorts of junk up there?" I said realising that I had very little to show Sam, only my comics and iPod and I was sure she would have them anyway. She seemed really grown up, much older than me, but she was so nice. Helping to rescue her had been lucky. If I hadn't, I wouldn't have met her.

"How do you get up there?"

"Watch. By the way, going up here is a bit of a secret. You won't tell Aunty M will you?"

"Course not, not if you don't want me to. Why is it such a secret?" asked Sam.

"I don't want her to know in case she stops me going up there. You know what grown ups are like don't you? She'll think I'll fall or whatever," I replied.

I cleared a space on the shelves and climbed up. I pulled the ring and hauled myself up. Sam followed.

"How cool is this," she remarked, "sort a secret room."

"That's what I thought the first time I came up here. I love it up here. Look."

I pointed to the rack of dressing up clothes. Then I took her down to the squashy sofa. My *Girl Talk* comic was still there but it was open at page three and I was sure I'd left it closed.

"Do you come up here and read? It's a bit spooky. Aren't you scared?"

"No. Well a bit I at first. I'm an only child so I'm always on my own. 'Spose I'm just used to it," I announced.

Above me in the rafters of the roof was a little 'phhh' sound and a sprinkle of dust showered my head. I think I said the wrong thing.

"Look at the time Florence. Mum will go mad. Tea at six and don't be late. It's tattooed on my heart! I must go but do you want to meet up again tomorrow?" asked Sam.

"Yes I would. Thanks for a great time," I said.

"What do you mean? What are you thanking me for? It's me who must thank you. Thank your aunt too for me, will you? She is a fantastic cake maker."

"I will. See you tomorrow."

"I'll come around at eleven. We'll go to check out my dinghy first and then we'll decide what to do for the rest of the day. Better wear old clothes because there will be cleaning on board to do."

Sam left and I waved goodbye from the door.

"You two seemed to get on very well. She has a fine appetite too," said Aunty M laughing

"She loved your cakes so we had a bit of all of them. We're meeting up tomorrow. I hope that is Ok."

"Course it is. I'm so pleased you have made a friend. Do you have lots of friends at home?" asked Aunty M.

"Eloise is my best friend at school and she comes for sleepovers. Mum hates sleepovers though so I don't ask her very often. There's a few other girls I like but because I'm so shy and I always think I'll say the wrong thing so I keep quiet. Best thing is though; Sam goes to St Maur's. How cool is that?"

Aunty Marmalade

"Never. Well I'll be blowed. What a coincidence. You'll have an instant friend there then. What good luck."

"Yes I know. She said she would be my 'shadow' and help me settle in. She's a year older than me so she'll be in the year above me."

"Now that's lucky too because the advice I was given by my mum was, 'get yourself an older, bigger friend and you can't go wrong!" said Aunty M laughing.

"Sounds like good advice," I agreed and we both laughed.

"But Florence, I've seen a change in you since you arrived. I don't think you'll be so shy from now on. And for goodness sake, stop worrying about saying the wrong thing. If you do, so what?"

"I know what you mean because I do feel different. I'm really going to try not to let the 'cool gang' get to me so much next term. I'm going to try to

stand up for myself more."

Chapter 19

Sam and I went to the Sailing Club the following day at eleven. Her dinghy, Bubblegum the Third, was on a stand along with other dinghies. It was dry but it needed to be cleaned out. We climbed inside it. We started filling Sam's black bin liners with the seaweed, stones and shells that were strewn all over the bottom of the boat. We pulled the sails out to let them dry out. Luckily, it was a sunny day.

"Thanks for your help with this. Mum said I can't take the boat out for a while. She thought I was a gonner!" said Sam laughing.

"Well it was a bit scary seeing you go over like that so I can understand what your mum means."

"Yes, it did shake me up a bit but I do love sailing. I can't wait to learn to drive. All that freedom. Just jump in the car and off you go. Sailing is like that…jump in the boat and sail away, but it is dangerous. The sea is dangerous."

"Do you want to come back for lunch? Aunty M said it is fine," I said.

When we arrived Aunty M was in the kitchen and she smiled at us saying,

"Hello girls. There's chicken gougons, chips and beans. Then there's strawberry cake with ice cream."

Sam and I looked at each other. We were both starving after working on the boat.

After lunch, we decided to go back up to the attic. First, we tried on some of the dresses.

Aunty Marmalade

"You look gorgeous, Sam. That hat looks simply divine," I said mimicking the lady on the fashion programme on TV.

"You look simply wonderful in that creation, Flo. The colour is perfect on you."

We both fell about laughing because we looked really silly. Sam wrapped a gruesome fox stole around her and paraded up to the end of the attic like she was on a catwalk. Then we sat down together on the sofa and looked through the window. Far below we could see the sea and Aunty M's garden.

"Sam, do you believe in ghosts?" I asked.

"No I don't. I think when you're dead you're dead. But some people do. My mum does."

"Really does she?" I said astounded that a grown up would.

"Yes. She says she's had some odd experiences when she feels she's being 'watched over.' That someone is sort of taking care of her. She's a bit religious so I guess that's the reason. Dad says it's a load of old twoddle and I sort of agree with him. Why do you ask?"

"No reason really," I said.

"Go on there must be a reason."

"No there isn't. Well at least I thought there might be, but Aunty M explained to me about being in old houses."

"I don't understand. What about being in old houses?"

"Well you know creaking floorboards, wind howling through the windows and doors slamming. You get all these noises in old houses. I live in a new house and the only noises we get are the London traffic. That's all you can hear."

"You live in London? That's cool. I'd love to live there. All those shops and restaurants and loads of things to do. There's not much going on down here. Anyway you thought you heard a ghost?" Sam continued.

"Yes I did. It seems daft now but it was a bit scary at the time."

"Well you weren't to know and you are in a strange house without your parents. Lord, look at the time. I've got a dentist appointment at four. Mum'll murder me if I'm late. Must dash."

That night as I lay in bed, I heard a click. I opened my eyes wondering what I was going to see and hear this time. There on the end of the bed was the girl. She looked just like me. She had a sort of white 'glow' around her and I could clearly see she was staring at me with those dead eyes, piercing through me. Terror shot through me and yet I could not stop staring. The way she looked at me made me feel cold and empty. I was shocked and frightened. I lay still as I could, unable to

110

breathe. I mustn't make a sound. I couldn't anyway.

Then she started to fade and I strained my eyes to keep her in view but as I blinked, she was gone.

Chapter 20

Sam and I met at the sailing club again the next day. We finished off clearing the boat and by the end, Sam said it looked as good as new. We went into the coffee bar and ordered two cokes and sat down. The door flung open suddenly and in came two boys of about thirteen or fourteen dressed in sailing gear.

"Hi Sam."

"Oh hi Pete. Hi Matt. This is Florence she's staying at Apple Jack's Cottage."

"Hi," they both said to me. I could feel my face getting hot and red. I smiled back too embarrassed to speak.

"You staying there for long?" asked Matt slumping into the chair.

"Just two weeks," I mumbled.

"Seen any ghosts yet?"

"Pardon?"

"You must have heard. That place is haunted. People always say they've been funny 'going ons' there."

"What sort of funny 'going ons'?" asked Sam.

"You know, the sort of things," answered Pete, "ghostly figures walking pass the window and in the garden in the moonlight."

"Flo, you thought you'd heard funny noises, didn't you?" said Sam.

"Yes, but it was only the old house noises. There are no ghosts there. Ghosts aren't real anyway." My face was burning and I knew my face must be red like a lobster now. In front of boys and Sam too. I felt

so stupid and babyish.

"Got you," the boys and Sam burst out laughing.

I had fallen for their stupid joke and rather than laugh

along with them, I hung my head in shame and wished I

could run away.

The boys got up and left.

"Flo, don't you know any boys?"

"No, it's all girls at my school. I feel so stupid.

They must think I'm a real dork."

"Don't worry; they think everyone's a dork

except them. They're Ok really. Just boys. My mum

says boys are a completely different species. I fancy

Matt which one do you fancy?"

I'd never even thought about boys in that way.

The only boy I ever really took any notice of was Dave

who was in a band called 'Scoop' up to that point, so I

didn't know what to say.

114

"Go on, which one Flo?"

"I don't know," I said totally embarrassed.

"Well, which one would you like to go out with?" asked Sam, with even more determination.

"Go out with? You're joking. My Mum would have a heart attack," I replied.

"No she wouldn't, bet you? She'd probably be pleased that boys fancy you."

"I doubt that. She still thinks I'm about four. I 'spose I prefer Pete but he wouldn't even notice me or possibly like me. Who'd fancy me with red hair and freckles?"

"Flo, you're gorgeous. Like that model what's her name? Only difference she's about two feet taller."

"Do you mean Lolly Middleham? I'm not remotely like her Sam."

"You just don't realise how pretty you are Flo."

Aunty Marmalade

Later on, I sat in my room looking at myself in the mirror. I tried to untangle my hair. Lolly Middleham, what a joke! I pouted and made a model face. Nope, I couldn't see any resemblance at all. But I did feel chuffed that Sam thought I was pretty. Apart from Aunty M and granny (and they didn't count because they would say things like that), no-one had ever told me I was pretty.

Behind me in the mirror, I saw the picture on the wall shift. Then the duvet and pillow started to ripple. Suddenly, the room became icy cold. I turned around. The ghost was there. She was glaring at me. She was clear and unmistakeable. It was like looking at me. The only difference was that she was pale and white, almost shiny. A glowing aura surrounded her. I froze. Petrified, I fell to the floor and covered my head in my arms.

"Get up, get up," she whispered at me.

"No, no leave me alone. Leave me alone. I can't bear this. I can't bear this. Please leave me alone. Why are you here? Why do you keep letting me see you? I don't want you. I want you to go away and leave me alone. I feel like I'm going mad."

"You're not. Get up. Get up now. I need you."

"No, no. Leave me alone. Go away and never come back. I can't help you," I said desperately.

"You can and you are the only one who can. I won't hurt you. I can't. I just need you to help me."

I unfolded my arms from my head and looked up. Tears were streaming down my face and my nose was running and I had to keep sniffing. God, mum would go mad if she could see me now. I looked up. The ghost was smiling at me now.

"Hello, Florence. I need your help. Will you help me?"

Aunty Marmalade

"How can I possibly help you? You're a ghost. Who are you? Please leave me alone. Can't you see that I am really scared? I am terrified of you."

"I know you are. I can see that, but I want you to help me rest in peace," said the ghost.

"How can I possibly help you? How could I help you 'rest in peace'?"

"But you are the only one. Don't say no, not ever. You're all I've got."

And with that, she faded away.

Chapter 21

Aunty M was digging in her vegetable plot the next day and was listening to some debate programme on the radio. Sam had gone out with her family and so I found myself alone. I decided to go up to the attic. For some strange reason, I felt sort of safe up there and I wanted to continue snooping about to see what else I could discover. In the back of my mind was a feeling that the ghost might visit me again up there. Well, that was where I heard the first noises. Feeling brave, I climbed the steps. Perhaps I would unearth some more clues to who was this 'ghost'. I had been thinking about what happened and what it said to me and the more I thought about it, the more I thought that I had dreamed it. For goodness sake, I didn't believe in ghosts. When you're dead, you're dead. Surely? So much was happening to me that I felt I was losing it. Or maybe she really did exist. I would not be so scared next time. I hoped.

I walked down to the sofa and sat down and waited. I picked up a huge, dusty old book from the bookcase. It was a book about birds. Each picture was beautifully painted and had a piece of grease proof paper to protect it. I turned over each page. I recognised some of the birds because I'd seen them on David Attenborough's programme on T.V. The book was so beautiful that at first, I didn't feel the temperature suddenly drop. I felt a cold waft of air trickle pass me. I looked around and felt a shiver run down my spine. I stared around feeling frightened and vulnerable. There was nothing. Nothing at all. I was getting flustered and spooked. The meeting with the ghost the day before really got to me. I felt my breathing slow down and go back to normal. I closed the book and carefully placed it back on the shelf. I couldn't stay up there alone. Not any more.

I turned towards the hatch. I couldn't wait to get out of the attic. Then as I strode to the steps, I heard a voice behind me.

"Wait. Please wait. Don't be afraid. I won't hurt you. I can't and I wouldn't even if I could. Just a minute. Can you wait just a minute?"

I stopped. I turned around slowly. I took a deep breath. There sitting on the sofa was the ghostly figure of someone who looked just like me. Her hair was long, ginger and untidy just like mine. She was dressed in the same white dress that I saw her in before. I could see right through her to the red velvet of the sofa. As she spoke, she floated up and drifted towards me. Then she hovered just in front of me. Her eyes were pleading me to wait. There was nothing I could do. I had to stop. I had to wait. I had to listen.

"Yes, I can wait. Aunty M is busy in the garden and I don't want to be in her way."

"I'm Roma your twin sister," she said.

"I don't think you can be my sister. I'm an only child. I'd know if I had a sister. I think you must have got it wrong."

"No there's no mistake. They never told you."

"Who never told me what?" I asked.

"Our mother, granny and granpy - that you had a sister, silly."

"But if that's true, why wouldn't they tell me. I don't understand. Why are there so many secrets?" I stammered.

"I'm not sure why they have never told you about me and dad. There must be another reason and I

don't know what that is. But I do know that I'm a
ghost," she stated.

"I know you are, but how did you die? I'm so
confused," I spluttered.

"You found the photos and the wedding dress,
didn't you? Then the christening dresses and the photo
of us when we were little."

"Yes, so you were watching me. I just don't
understand why there's you and me and mum with that
other man. And why is mum married to someone else?
Where's our real dad, for goodness sake? I'm so
muddled up and I don't know who to ask to tell me the
truth."

"I can only tell you my part of the story. Our
dad is the man in the photo but I don't know what
happened to him. You will have to ask Aunty M about
that."

Aunty Marmalade

"Aunty M? Yes, I suppose she'd be easier to tackle than mum. After all, it's mum who is keeping all these secrets," I said.

I wanted to know there and then. All these secrets that I knew nothing about and they all involved me. Tears started to well up in my eyes. Here I was in the attic talking to the ghost of my dead twin and I wasn't dreaming; this was for real.

"So what happened to you, Roma?" I demanded.

"When we were about six months old, I became poorly. We were alone with mum and dad wasn't there. I don't know where he was. Mum was frantic about me and she called a taxi. I must have been very ill because we all rushed to hospital where I died alone with just a nurse looking after me. Mum couldn't stay with me because there was no-one to look after you. So I died in the arms of the nurse who didn't know me. I never had

124

the chance to see you again, never said goodbye to mum or dad. So I'm stuck here. I couldn't get into heaven until now. Because you are here I can go, because I couldn't 'rest in peace' until we said goodbye and you found out about me and dad."

I stood speechless then stammered, "But you've grown up like me. How can that be?"

"I've always been here. I have lived here with Aunty M all along. I don't know why I'm here and not with you. I don't remember the reason but there must be one. There are lots of things that I don't remember. I don't seem to be able to remember like you would. Perhaps that's the trouble with being a ghost. I did see you in London a few times because I travelled up there with Aunty M. I'm not sure why. I stopped you walking out in front of that car that day. You could have been killed."

Aunty Marmalade

"You were the one that saved me. I had a feeling that I had a guardian angel," I said astounded. "I've had a feeling that someone was watching over me."

"Yep, that was me. Not all the time though until now. I only 'helped' when you were in trouble. Remember when that horrible girl in the 'cool gang' called you names and pushed you? What was her name?" asked Roma.

"Oh yes, Georgia. I hate her," I said then regretting that I'd used the word, 'hate'. Well I did 'hate' her, but it sounded awful saying it out loud.

"Well remember the day her dress got stuck in her knickers?"

I nodded, "Omigod. That was you?"

"Sure was. Great, wasn't it! I just had to do something to give her some of her own medicine so I just sort of did it! I had a right laugh about that," said Roma laughing.

"Yeah, so did I," I replied laughing too.

"Did I scare you when I messed up your room and made those noises the other day?"

"I was scared at first but Aunty M said the house is noisy, so I sort of thought it was that and I guessed I must have forgotten to tidy my room in the morning but I knew I had, so I was just confused. I never thought there was a ghost. I've been more worried about the man in the photo. Is he our dad?"

"Yes. But I don't know where he is or what happened to him."

"Neither do I. I wish none of this had happened to you. It's so unfair."

"I know. I wish that things were different but they aren't."

Aunty Marmalade

"Florence, want a cuppa?" came Aunty M's
voice calling up the stairs.

"That's Aunty M. I'd better go. Shall we talk
again tomorrow? Coming Aunty M."

"See you tomorrow," said Roma.

And she faded away to nothing.

"Thought you'd like a cup of tea, dear. Are you
alright Florence?"

"I'm fine. Yes fine. I'm writing the dreaded
diary and stuff."

I was pleased she didn't ask me what the 'and
stuff' meant. As I sipped my tea, I realised that Aunty
M probably knew everything. All I had to do was ask
her. I couldn't pluck up the courage. Well, not yet
anyway.

Chapter 22

"Was it you that rescued me and Biggles from the sea?" I asked Roma the following day.

"Yes, I was following you around and then I realised you couldn't get out of the sea, so I sort of dragged you out and Biggles too."

"Why did you mess up my room?"

"Sorry about that but you had put that music thing away and I wanted to try it, so I had to find it. I'm not tidy like you."

"That's my iPod. Do you want to listen now?"

"Can I?" said Roma excitedly.

"Sure." I pulled it out of my pocket and held up the earphones. Roma took them and placed them where her ears were but as she was not 'real' they only sort of sat where her ears would have been. They looked like they were hanging. It looked really weird.

"What's funny Florence?"

"Sorry, it's just that I have just realised that you are…" I couldn't think of the right word.

"A spirit, a ghost. I know. Don't worry I'm quite used to it."

I pressed the start button on. Roma winced and then started tapping her feet.

"Do you like it?" I asked.

"Yes it's frozen," she said.

"I think you mean cool or hot!"

"Yeah, that as well."

She gently removed the earphones. "I have a confession to make Florence."

130

"What?" I asked again.

"The painting of the twins. I stole it from a car boot sale in the village. I saw it and recognised our great, great granny and her sister. Aunty M was right, it had been sold by accident and I sort of brought it back to where it belongs. It was a sign to you that we should be together again. It helped didn't it because here we are."

"Well don't worry, I won't tell anyone." And we both giggled.

I looked into her eyes. They were hazy but I could still see they were blue like mine. A desperate feeling of sadness came over me and I realised how awful this situation was. There was nothing I could do to help her. Nothing at all. All she wanted me to do was help her rest in peace. All I wanted to do was make her come alive again so we could stay as twin sisters.

Aunty Marmalade

Without realising it, tears were streaming down my cheeks and I couldn't stop them.

"Why are you crying?" Roma asked suddenly distressed.

"It's so unfair. Why did you have to die? We could have such fun together. I'm always so lonely. I find making friends hard as I think people think I'm stupid and I never know the right things to say."

"But you got on with Sam Ok, didn't you?"

"Yes, but she's such an easy sort of person to get along with. You should have seen me with these two boys Pete and Matt yesterday."

"I did," announced Roma.

"You did?"

"Yup, I've been following you everywhere. I'm trying to learn about your world before I have to go."

"You don't have to 'go' soon though do you?" I asked.

"No. I can stay for a while but I really do have to get myself settled because as the days go by, I can feel a tiredness coming over me. That is the sign that I'm being 'called.' It's what happens. I can't hang around forever. You get 'called' you see."

"Who calls you? Who wants you to go?" I asked desperately.

"The people who have gone before us. They want me to join them and to rest in peace."

"I bet they do but I don't want you to. I want you to stay with me," I pleaded.

"That's not possible, Florence."

"Well I might not be here if it wasn't for you. I could have drowned."

"Yes I know. I was a bit naughty there I shouldn't have got involved, but I couldn't let you drown even though I wanted you to."

"Really?" I said astounded.

"Of course I wanted you to drown because then we could be together forever. Then I realised that it was unfair and that I wanted you to have every chance to live. I was being very selfish," said Roma.

"Thank you for what you did for Biggles and me."

"Have you realised we have real grandparents. Our real dad's parents. You need to meet them. We need to bring the family back together. There was a big upset before we were born and I'm not sure what happened. Our real dad's parents don't know you. Once the upset is mended, I can go."

"I never knew about them. I thought my dad was my dad. Now I know he isn't," I said.

I stood up and tried to put my arms around her but of course I couldn't because she was only a spirit. She faded away until there was nothing left. I exhausted her obviously and as I slumped back into the sofa, I realised how tired I was myself. But she was right. We did have grandparents that we had never met. Why was our real dad such a secret? Why did mum not tell me she was married before? I knew then that I had to do something and I had to do it quickly for Roma.

Chapter 23

The next day, I decided that I would have to do something positive about my situation. I would have to pluck up courage and ask Aunty M. It would take guts and I really didn't know whether I had enough courage to ask her. I decided not to plan anything. Just see how things went at the time. We got on really well together and I felt pretty confident she wouldn't mind. I just couldn't bear not knowing. I needed answers. I needed to know who I really was. I wasn't sure any more.

I was sitting at the table having hot chocolate; steam was spilling out of my mug.

"Aunty M can I ask you something?"

"Yes my dear. Anything."

"Can I ask you something? I'm a bit worried about asking you but you're the only one I can ask."

"Go on anything Flo. We know each other now so well. If I can help you I will and if I can't I won't."

"I found some old Victorian stuff in the attic."

"You've been up in the attic? "said Aunty M staring at me crossly.

"Yes I have. I found the secret stairway and I went up to look. I wondered if I could take some of the stuff I found for my project on the Victorian's at school."

"Florence, why did you not tell me before about finding the way up there? Is that what you were doing the night you fell?"

I nodded ashamed of myself.

Aunty Marmalade

"There are a lot of private things up there you know. You should have asked me first. I am a little surprised at you."

"Aunty M, I am so sorry. I didn't realise that I could upset you by going up. I just read and stuff up there," I replied, feeling absolutely wretched.

"Anyway, what did you find?" continued Aunty M.

I chickened out. What would I do if she refused to tell me or I embarrassed her or hurt her feelings? Suddenly I realised that what I had found out she might not know about or feel she should be the one to tell me if she did know. Was it really any of my business?

"I found some old toys; a wooden top and a push-along-horse."

"Yes that's fine. I think you had better bring them back once your project is finished but that's fine. They've been in the family for years so I suppose they better stay at Apple Jack's Cottage, but its fine for you to borrow them. Are you sure that that is all you want to take?"

"Yes that's all."

Go on; go on ask her then I found myself saying,

"Aunty M?"

"Yes, Florence. Is there something else?"

"Yes there is but I don't know how to say it to you because I realise I've upset you so much. I did not realise until now what I have done. I wouldn't upset you for the world."

"Say what darling?" said Aunty M.

"Well it's like this."

"What's that sweetie?" asked Aunty M staring at me straight in the face.

Then from somewhere, I got the courage.

"I found some old photos and a wedding dress."

Aunty Marmalade

"Oh, you found them did you? How on earth did you find them?"

"Yes I did. I found them quite by accident. I found the christening gowns too. They must have been for my great, great grandma and her sister."

"You found those too did you?"

"My mum was wearing the wedding dress in the photo but she wasn't marrying dad she was marrying someone else. I don't know who he is because he's not my dad."

"Is all this something to do with why mum doesn't like me?"

"Florence, she doesn't not like you; she's just cold and unfeeling. She's always been the same. She's that kind of person. Let me tell you what happened and then maybe you'll be able to understand better. Things did happen that made her feel the way she does but she doesn't blame you. None of this was your fault my

dear. You were only a baby."

"So I am involved then. I guessed that."

"Come on, let's go and sit in a comfortable

chair. Florence, this is going to be a bit difficult for me

but I'll try to tell you as much as I feel I can. I don't

want to upset mum or granny or anyone come to it."

So I sat there with Aunty M and she told me the

story about mum, dad, and me and Roma and it made

all the pieces of the jigsaw fit. The curtain behind

Aunty M flicked up and down a bit and I knew that

Roma was there in the room with us. Even if I hadn't

seen the curtain move, I would have known she was

there. I had become so close to her.

Chapter 24

"Your mum and dad met at university. They started to go out and after a very short time they decided to get married. They were very young". She took a deep breath and continued, "Granny and granpy liked him very much and even though they thought it was all a bit quick, they gave their consent and as soon as they had left university they got married. Simon was supposed to marry a friend of his family. His parents were furious, and did not give their blessing to the marriage and that created a very bad atmosphere between them all. But, nevertheless, it was a lovely wedding, a very happy day. They went on honeymoon and returned to their little house in Tarlton to be near Simon's parents and granny and granpy. Simon's parents didn't make the situation very easy. They continued to make your mum's life very difficult. They made no attempts to get on with her."

"Poor mum, it must have been very difficult for her. What happened then?" I asked eager for the story to continue.

"Hang on, I'm getting there."

"The next thing was really very exciting because your mum and dad found out they were going to have a baby. Everyone was excited of course except Simon's parents. They continued to feel that he was far too young to be a father. He hadn't got his career established yet. But new babies in families are always very exciting; then they discovered they were going to have twins."

Aunty Marmalade

"They were having twins," I repeated. I felt my jaw drop down. My hands felt all sweaty and my throat became dry.

"They were having twins," Aunty M repeated, "Our family was ecstatic. Not one baby but two, what could be better?"

I tried to say something but I couldn't seem to say anything the words wouldn't come out. The curtain shook violently behind Aunty M. Roma and I now knew who our father was and I now knew that the man that I called dad was not my dad or Roma's dad after all. I felt the colour drain from my face.

"Are you alright dear? You've gone rather pale."

"I'm fine, Aunty M," I said. But I couldn't believe what I was hearing.

"Simon became very concerned with his parents behaviour and decided he could not let the situation

144

continue. What was worrying him more was that your mum was getting very upset and this was not good for her or the two babies."

"So one night after he finished at his lawyer's practice," continued Aunty M, "he didn't go home but went shopping. He bought two huge teddies for the new babies and drove straight to his parent's house. He wanted to try to make them see sense. He even took the teddies inside with him probably to make them realise there was nothing he could do he was in love with your mum and there were two new little babies coming into the family."

"What happened? Bet they realised they were being stupid," I couldn't believe this story as it was unfolding, but the worse was to come.

"There was a terrible argument. They wouldn't listen or even try to understand so Simon stormed out of the house. The police found his crashed car in the woods. He had skidded off the wet road and hit a tree. He died instantly they said, all alone."

"What happened to mum?" I asked horrified.

"She was frantic when he did not come home from work. She had phoned his office and got no answer. She phoned granpy and he went around to their house and he decided that the police would have to be called."

"They found the teddies in the front seat. Simon had even put the seat belt around them. He was on the road just down the road from his parent's house. It was a tragic accident."

"So Simon died before the babies were born. They never knew their dad. He never saw his own babies. This is the saddest story I have ever heard," I felt the tears trickle down my face and I had to blow my nose.

"Your mum was too ill to go to the funeral. It was probably for the best as it had been Simon's parents who were to blame in some ways for the accident."

"If he hadn't gone to try to talk to them, it never would have happened, would it?"

"We'll never know Florence. But if he hadn't gone that night he could still be alive."

"When were the twins born?"

"Two little girls were born on the 24th March."

"That's the same date as my birthday."

"Yes Florence. Simon was your father. You look very similar to him you know. He was dark, you get the red hair from our side of the family, but you have his eyes and the gap between your front teeth just like him. Do you know too, you are so like him in so many ways? Very kind, quiet and gentle. You are a real credit to him you know."

Aunty Marmalade

"But I have a twin sister too. What happened to her?" I knew of course but I had to protect Roma and Roma didn't know the entire story either.

"She became ill when you were just six months old and died in hospital. She was not a strong little baby like you. Mum blamed all the upset over Simon's death. Your mum was very poorly before you were born."

"Where is my twin sister buried?"

"She's buried in the churchyard here in Tarlton in Saint Luke's Church. Would you like to visit it?"

"Yes I would. Can we go first thing in the morning?"

"Sure and we'll take some flowers too. I haven't been since you came down."

"Do you go there often?"

"Yes I do, every week. I always take her some flowers."

"Aunty M?"

"Yes dear."

"I just realised. I have a dad who isn't my dad. I have grandparents who aren't really my grandparents and I have grandparents that I have never met. How spooky is that?"

"Good and spooky Florence. Good and spooky."

"Aunty M, I just can't believe what has happened to my dad, my sister and my mum." I could feel the back of my throat start to choke and the tears pouring down my face, "I just can't believe mum and dad never said anything to me. Why didn't they?"

"Florence, you know what grown ups are like with their secrets. We all have secrets and sometimes we can't find it in us to share them. Sometimes even adults find telling the truth hard, particularly if they've done something silly. I don't think any of us wanted you to be upset and hurt by what happened. I was worried about telling you and to be honest, I think I may have said too much. Granny will probably disown me and as for your mum, she'll never forgive me. The family thought you might never find out and that it would all be for the best. Trust it to be me that ends up being the one that tells you. If only I could turn back the clock. If only things had been different. Florence, will you ever be able to forgive me?"

"What do you mean? You've done nothing, Aunty M."

Then to my horror, I saw tears streaming down Aunty M's face. She pulled out a huge red and white spotty hankie from the pocket of her floral tent dress and blew her nose. I once heard granny say that when Aunty M blew her nose it sounded like the Queen Mary ship sounding her horn leaving for a voyage and I now knew what she meant. But now was not a time to laugh. Aunty M got up and quietly walked out of the room.

I sat for a while trying to make sense of what I had heard. I was surprised that she got so upset when she was not really that involved. The door slammed shut and I guessed that Roma had left the room too. Could ghosts cry? I didn't know. But I knew then and there that I had to get in touch with my real grandparents. I wanted to get to know them; they were part of me. They could be a way of connecting with my real father. And I had to do it soon.

Chapter 25

I went up to bed. As I lay there I thought about
all that had happened. I thought back to the wedding
photos of my mum and Simon. He had looked so
familiar and yet I didn't know him. I looked a little bit
like him. What I couldn't get out of my head was I had
grandparents that I did not know I had until today. I
hadn't thought of that before. There were people in my
family that I didn't even know about - new people that
in a funny sort of way could bring my dad, my real dad,
closer to me. I felt so sad, so full of odd feelings. How
could I miss someone I had never known? And yet I
did, I really did. I couldn't bear the feelings any longer,

so I climbed the steps to the attic. I needed to look back at the photo album and see if I could get any clues as to my father's family name.

I clutched the album and turned the pages until I came to the wedding pictures. There was Simon, my dad. Now I could see what Aunty M meant because he was handsome.

I turned the page and there was the photo of mum, Simon, granny and granpy. On the other side of Mum were two people. They must be Simon's parents. I stared at them. They looked normal and nice. They looked just like any grandparents would look. I wondered what they knew about me. Did they know anything about me? Anything at all?

Wonder what they're like? Why haven't they tried to meet me? They must be awful because of what they did to mum and Simon yet they didn't look bad or evil or anything. I was so interested in them. Under the photo someone had written, "Rosamund and Alistair Rhodes, June and Henry Masters."

So my grandparents name was Rhodes, not a very common name. I knew they must live locally because Aunty M said they did. How could I find out? The phone book. I could look in the phone book. Simple. I just hoped they were not ex-directory.

I closed my eyes and as I opened them there was Roma standing in front of me. She looked paler than I had ever seen her. I could see the bookcase behind her. She was smiling.

"Going to my grave tomorrow then?"

"Yes. So you heard the story. Dad died before we were born."

"Yes, I can't believe it. That explains why mum was on her own when I became poorly that night. She was coping all alone with the two of us. That's why I was left at the hospital. Granny and granpy must have been away. I wonder where Aunty M was."

"I wonder if that's why mum is sort of like she is. She's just never got over Simon and you dying and she sort of blames me because I lived and you both didn't. Then she married Philip, dad, but she never got over what happened because I remind her all the time," I said realising that I was probably right.

"She can't be that silly. It wasn't your fault," said Roma reassuringly.

"No it was nobody's fault. But she gets so cross with me all the time I just feel I must be to blame for some of it. It must have been hard for mum."

"Yes and hard for you. Our dad is not our dad either. What are you going to say to him?" asked Roma with a shrug.

"I'm not going to say anything to anyone. I'm certainly not going to ask mum, she'll be furious I've asked Aunty M about her and what happened and I've been snooping around. I've done everything she told me not to do. She'll never speak to me again."

"Course she will."

"You don't know our mum. She's pretty fierce. I'm terrified of her and I don't want to make matters worse."

"What about Aunty M?"

"I don't think she'll say anything unless I ask her to. I've spent eleven years not knowing, so the secret can stay for a while longer until I can pluck up the courage to tell mum I know when I'm about forty five."

"Forty five!?" giggled Roma.

"Yeah, it will take me that long at least."

"I'm going to find out the address of our real grandparents, Roma."

"Are you sure you don't mind doing this for me. They've never made any attempts at trying to find you or see you. They might be rude and upset you. They might refuse to see you. You may cause a lot of trouble, Flo," said Roma with feeling.

"I know but I can't not find them now. I want to try to get to know our real dad. I think it's just something I need to do. If you need help to 'rest in peace', we need to get everyone back together again and try to what's that saying; 'bury the bucket'?"

"That doesn't sound right Flo, but anyway I think you're right, we need to get everyone together so we can all say 'sorry' and forget what's happened."

"Yes, I want to meet them really badly. I just can't imagine what they are like. It's exciting really to meet new people in your family that you never knew about. Like you really. I have a sister that I knew nothing about. I just wish you didn't have to go away.

157

Aunty Marmalade

Why do you have to 'rest in peace'? Why can't we just carry on like this?" I asked, thinking it was all so simple.

"I have to go. They are calling me and telling me to hurry."

"Who are 'they'?" I asked puzzled.

"They are our ancestors. It is their job to protect us once we die. I have to go, otherwise I will be lost forever nowhere and I've been told that is the worse thing that can happen to any spirit or ghost. I need to get there because I don't want to end up 'nowhere.' I want to be with them. Have you noticed I seem to be getting paler?"

I realised that this must be the sign that she was losing her chance to 'rest in peace.' I would have to work quickly. I would have to do whatever I could for her. I was the lucky one. I had lived.

Roma disappeared and I went back down to bed. I couldn't sleep at first as my head was buzzing with everything. First thing tomorrow, I would get the phone book, find their address and phone number and write to my new grandparents. I wouldn't tell Aunty M and I would face whatever happened. I had to get the family back together for Roma. And with that thought, I relaxed and let sleep take me through night's journey.

Chapter 26

The seagulls' screeching woke me very early

the next morning. I opened my eyes and stretched

remembering what I had to do. I tiptoed to the bedroom

door and opened it. It clicked open. There was silence.

Aunty M was still in her room. Biggles was still in his

bed downstairs.

I crept down the stairs and turned into the study

off the hall. I found the phone book and flicked through

to the 'Rs'. I ran my finger down the pages until I

landed on 'Rhodes.' There were only four names.

There, to my absolute relief was;

Rhodes A. Willow tree House, Willow Tree Lane, Tarlton.

I scribbled the address and phone number down on one of Aunty M's 'post it' notes. I knew where they lived. Tarlton was only a small place and the lane they lived on was further down the coast road on the right. I had passed the end of their lane when Sam and I went to the sailing club. I remembered thinking at the time what a lovely name for a road. A thought struck me that it was possible I had already seen them at the shops or on the beach. I marched out of the room and set off back upstairs. Behind me, I heard a noise: click, click, click, whoosh. I slowly turned around and to my horror; there was Biggles and Aunty M standing at the foot of the stairs.

"You're up early Flo. Everything alright?"

"Yes, fine," I stuttered feeling my face flush bright red.

Aunty Marmalade

I couldn't think of an excuse so I turned back and continued back up the stairs, hoping Aunty M wouldn't ask me what I had been doing.

I quickly opened the dressing table drawer where I'd seen some writing paper and envelopes. I put the address and the date at the top and started to write. I wanted to get the letter written and posted straight away.

My pen hovered over the page and I wrote; "My name is Florence and I am your granddaughter. I have only just found out about you and I would very much like to meet you. My mobile number is 07986 243562. If you would like to meet me, could you please call me on this number and I will come to visit you. I am staying with my godmother in Tarlton until the 24th October."

I ended the letter with best wishes Florence Masters. I decided not to put a kiss because I didn't know them yet. I found a stamp in my purse. I bought six stamps at the post office because mum had told me to, just in case I wrote to granny or my friend Eloise. She didn't want me pestering Aunty M.

After breakfast we bought some flowers in the mini mart and walked to the little graveyard in the grounds of St Luke's church.

"Seems so strange seeing where my sister is buried. If only she was still here."

"How many times I have said that Florence? It would have been easier for you and your mum if there had been the two of you to care for and she would have found losing Simon a little easier somehow. It's all so sad."

"You could be right, Aunty M. And there's dad, I mean Philip."

"Philip? You mean your dad?" asked Aunty M.

"No Philip; he's not my real dad after all."

Aunty Marmalade

"Florence, he's been your dad and he's been wonderful to you and your mum."

"I know Aunty M but he's not my real, dad is he?"

"No, but he married mum when you were only about a year old and he has loved you and cared for you just like your real dad would have done. Mum was very lucky when she met him. We are all so very fond of him and he loves you very much. You only have to watch him with you to see that."

"Yes I know but I'm feeling very muddled up Aunty M. Everything is different now."

"You know what happened to you and mum but nothing has changed really. You'll be fine and so will mum and Philip. You've just grown up a bit, well a big bit."

Aunty M walked away towards the entrance gate. I bent down and place the bunch of flowers in the little container. I stood up and looked at the headstone.

It said, "Roma Masters 1996".

"Our Little Angel fell asleep when she was just

six months old.

Rest in Peace Little One."

If only you all knew, I thought. Their 'Little

One' could not 'rest in peace' until they all met and

forgave each other for what happened years before. I

really was growing up quickly. I was learning how

grown ups could let you down. Feeling desperate, I ran

down the path to join Aunty M.

Chapter 27

Two days later, after lunch, when I was writing

my diary and gazing out of the window at the fishing

boats bobbing about on the waves, my phone rang. My

heart stopped. I had been willing my phone to ring as I

guessed that my letter was delivered the day before. I

posted it when Aunty M popped into the Mini Mart to

buy some onions. She never asked me what I was doing

in the study two mornings before. She was amazing.

She treated me like a grown up and never asked

questions. I couldn't tell whether she was disinterested

or whether she was giving me privacy. I decided to

believe it was the latter. She knew I needed space to be myself. Well on this occasion, I was glad she did.

I flicked up my phone.

"Hello."

"Hello is that Florence?"

"Yes it is who's speaking?"

"This is your grandma, Rosamund and your grandfather, Alastair, is next to me."

"Oh my goodness," I heard myself saying, "how do you do?"

"We are fine and very keen to meet you. When would you be able to visit?"

"I could come to see you tomorrow. You are only about fifteen minutes away from where I am staying. I can walk quite easily."

"Yes you can. Why don't you come for tea tomorrow, say at four?"

Aunty Marmalade

"I'd like that very much. See you at four then," I responded.

"We are looking forward to meeting you. Goodbye."

"Goodbye grandma."

My phone went dead.

I sat on my bed my heart pounding. I started now and I would have to go on. I was excited and yet deeply worried that I would cause more trouble with my mum and Aunty M. I felt really bad about the attic and how I upset Aunty M so badly. There were so many secrets and no-one made any attempts to tell me. My mum was always so sharp and irritated with me and I never knew why. And most important of all was Roma who needed us all.

"Who was that?" came a voice behind me.

I swung around hoping it was not Aunty M. It was Roma.

"That was our real grandparents. I'm seeing them tomorrow at four for tea. Will you come too?"

"Sure. I wouldn't miss meeting them for anything," said Roma as she hovered above my bed.

I looked at her and as I did I realised time was running out. She was very pale and her eyes, which had been bright blue, were losing their glint.

I know I had to work fast. Mum and Philip would be back at the weekend. They were coming down to collect me on Sunday. I had three days to make a miracle happen. It was a risk I knew I had to take, and with that thought, I went downstairs to see if Aunty M would like a cup of tea. Everything would have to be normal. I could not raise any suspicions. I would have to lie about where I was going tomorrow; I knew that but I felt it was the right thing to do. I had to do all I could to save my sister Roma.

Aunty Marmalade

Chapter 28

Aunty M was busy painting and I wasn't really sure she listened to my excuse that I was going out to tea at Sam's house. She smiled and waved her paint brush at me and muttered something about not being too late and that we were having sticky toffee pudding for tea. As I was scurrying towards my grandparent's house I tittered to myself. I could see mum glaring at me and saying, "Florence, don't forget what I told you. I don't want you coming home overweight after eating all those ridiculous puddings she insists on making. She's always had a sweet tooth and I don't want you following in her footsteps. To be overweight is a terrible thing and very bad for your health. It's also

very embarrassing and I DO NOT want to be

embarrassed by you." It felt like my tummy was

writhing with snakes as it was. I could clearly see my

mum's grey eyes piercing through me. Well, anyway I

was alright so far I reckoned. My clothes felt the same

not tight or anything.

As I strode along the road, I hummed, "One step

nearer, one step nearer." I was excited but so nervous.

What I was doing was the right thing I knew that but

the consequences, terrified me. If it all went wrong,

mum would never talk to me again. I was more worried

about upsetting Aunty M. I couldn't really explain why.

She was so kind to me. She made me feel like I

mattered and what I said was relevant and important. I

had never had so much freedom either. Staying with

Aunty M was the best time I had ever had. I realised

there and then as I skipped along the road that I hadn't

missed my mum at all. In fact, I hardly thought about her. Philip was away so much that I was used to being without him all the time. He was fun when he was at home, but of course, now it would all be different. I knew he was not my dad; well not my real dad. I had unearthed so many secrets and so far no-one knew, I knew.

I turned down Walnut Tree Lane. Half-way down, I came to their house. It had huge wrought iron gates and a gravel drive up to the front door. It was a large and very lovely house with a beautiful front garden full of trees and bushes.

I stopped and looked up at the house. As I raised my hand up to the doorbell, the door opened. There, standing on the doorstep were two elderly people smiling down at me.

"Hello, I'm Florence."

"Hello, welcome. Please come in."

They stood aside and I walked into the hall.
Grandpa held out his hand and I did the same and he
shook my hand and smiled. Grandma then did the same.
I followed them into the sitting room. Grandpa pointed
to a chair and I sat down. I wanted to give a good
impression of myself. I wanted to show them that mum
had done a good job of bringing me up.

"Florence, we are truly delighted to meet you. If
you only knew how often we speak about you. We
wondered what you looked like and what you are doing.
How are you and your family?" asked my grandma.

"I am very well, thank you, and my entire
family are well. I am staying with Aunty Marmalade
because my parents are on a business trip to Australia,"
I replied.

"Who is Aunty Marmalade? I don't think we
know who she is, do we Alistair?" said my grandma.

"She is my godmother, grandma. My mum's sister Madeleine."

"Oh, oh, yes I remember." said grandma stuttering. And how is your mother?"

"She is very well, thank you. She's very busy though. She's always busy," I said.

"And your grandparents?"

"They are fine. They are always going on holiday because granpy is retired now."

"Good for them. And how about you? We want to know all about you."

I told them about school and that I was going to boarding school in September. I told them about the subjects I liked, the sports I played and the 'cool gang' that made my life a misery.

Grandma and grandpa got up to collect the tea things. I lay the napkin they gave me on my lap and said I would just like milk in my tea. I chose some tiny

174

ham sandwiches and put them on my plate and a little pastry too. When I finished I put my tea things on the tray, folded my napkin and lay it down on the tray too.

"We would like to know how you came to want to see us Florence," said my grandma. "We tried to get in touch with you many times but I'm afraid your mother refused any contact with you and so we gave up trying. There was a lot of bad feeling all those years ago."

"I only found out about you recently," I answered, "I didn't know about my real dad."

Grandma put her hands up to her face and stared at me in disbelief. Grandpa shook his head.

I told them how I found out and that I had not told anyone. I didn't say anything about Roma, of course. I could see the sadness in their eyes.

"How do you feel now you know, Florence?" asked grandpa.

Aunty Marmalade

"I'm a bit confused really. You see I didn't know I had a twin sister either. I just can't understand why no-one ever told me."

"So no-one in your family knows you are visiting us today?" said grandma in disbelief.

"No. I haven't told anyone. I just didn't want to tell in case they stopped me. I mean it is my business if you think about it. I feel a bit cross and hurt but at the same time, I don't want to upset anyone. They must have had their reasons I suppose," I exclaimed.

"You look very like your father," commented my grandma. "He was a wonderful, talented son and we miss him terribly. You have his eyes, the gap between your teeth and his kind and gentle manner. This is a wonderful day for us, our dear sweet girl. We hope that now we have met you, you will keep in touch with us. We want to get to know you better and be part of your life, if you would let us."

"I want that more than anything else," I replied,

and with that I jumped up and threw my arms around

them both. They were two lonely, old people with no-

one. But now, they had me. I was going to bring

everyone back together. They would become part of my

life, whatever the cost.

Chapter 29

Later, I lay on my bed looking at the ceiling. I was trying to make sense of all that happened to me since I arrived at Aunty M's. I heard a thud coming from the attic. Must be Roma. I climbed the steps and pulled myself into the attic. I could see Roma sitting on the sofa with my mobile phone.

"Hi there," I said, "how are things? Why didn't you come to meet our grandparents?"

"Hi Florence. Sorry I couldn't. I haven't been feeling too good today. I'm finding it harder and harder to move. I really don't feel the same as I did. Time is running out for me. Anyway what happened?"

"They are really great. They have wanted to get in touch with me for ages but the family wouldn't let them have any contact with me. They were pretty surprised that I got in touch with them. I had to tell them how I found out."

"What did they think? Did you tell them about me?" asked Roma.

"No of course I didn't. Well I couldn't, could I? I wanted to, but I don't think they would believe me. Well I hardly believe myself! Now I have to decide what to do next. I know I've got to do something quickly. Mum and dad are back on Saturday, that's just two days away."

"Florence, what are you doing up there? Who are you speaking to?" came a voice from my room below.

"Omigod it's Aunty M. What am I going to say?" I whispered.

Aunty Marmalade

"I don't know Florence."

And she melted away.

"Coming Aunty M," I called.

I walked to the hatch and peered down. Aunty M was standing looking up towards the hatch. She had her hands on her hips and she didn't look happy.

Chapter 30

I took a deep breath and climbed down the steps. I couldn't think straight. I couldn't think of an excuse. I didn't want to lie. I had lied enough already. Time was running out for Roma, so I decided there and then to tell the truth.

"Florence, what are you doing up there again and who on earth are you talking to?" asked Aunty M.

"I was sort of talking to myself Aunty M. I'm sorry about going up to the attic again. I just went up to collect a few things I left up there," I said going red.

"What things, Florence?" she said exasperated.

"Just magazines, Aunty M."

Aunty Marmalade

"I think we had better talk Florence. I am rather disappointed you didn't tell you were still going up there. Why on earth didn't you tell me? You know there are things up there that are private and my business. We had better go and sit down together."

I followed her downstairs and we sat in the kitchen.

"I went to see my dad's parents today, Aunty M."

"You went to see Simon's parents today? You did what?" said Aunty M and she put her head in her hands. "What happened, Florence?"

"They were lovely and told me they had tried to get in touch with me but it had not been possible. They only live a short way from here," I said.

"I know they do Florence. Oh dear, what a mess all this is. What have I done to you? What have we all done to you?" muttered Aunty M.

"I was worried about telling you Aunty M, and I'm petrified of mum finding out," I said.

"I now know that you should have been told about Simon and Roma but the family was trying to protect you. It was just easier to let you think that you had been the only baby and that Philip was your dad. It was a decision that the family made. I just went along with everything. Everyone blamed Simon's parents for Simon and Roma's death. It wasn't their fault directly, of course, but they were against the marriage all along. I supposed everyone thought it would never come out, that you would never find out. I guessed it would. You can't keep secrets forever. You will need to discuss all this with mum when she comes on Saturday," finished Aunty M. Then without saying anything else, she got up and walked out fumbling in her pocket for her hankie.

Aunty Marmalade

Seconds later, I heard her talking on the phone to someone. I guessed it was granny. I went up to my room. I realised I had upset Aunty M again by sneaking behind her back. I would never forgive myself for what I had done. I couldn't tell them that I was on a rescue mission for Roma, that we needed to get together to say sorry and then she could rest in peace. That was a secret I would never tell and I would have to face the consequences. I would have to be brave for my sister.

Chapter 31

Aunty M said nothing about what I had done over dinner, except that mum and Philip were coming to collect me on Saturday morning, and that granny and granpy were also coming to see them. This surprised me because I had a return ticket for the train; they were not supposed to come down for me. This was getting a bit serious. Aunty M didn't know about the family gathering to help Roma and yet she was helping Roma and me without knowing. I couldn't believe my luck. She chatted away, just like always, and she had made chocolate profiteroles filled with cream and smothered in oozing, chocolate sauce for pudding. All I needed now was to get my grandma and grandpa here too, and I would have everyone in place for Roma.

Later on as I lay in bed, I thought about what I should do. I would have to be really brave if I was to ask my grandma and grandpa to Apple Jack's Cottage without permission. If I asked Aunty M first she might say *no,* then what would I do? No, it seemed to me that I would have to suffer the consequences for Roma's sake. It would be worth it; it had to be.

The moonlight filtered through the curtains throwing a shaft of light on the wall in front of me. The wind whispered through the cracks around the window frame. I had got so used to being in this room. I loved it. I loved its cosiness and the way it seemed to protect me. I could feel a wave of dread wash over me. I really didn't want to go home. It seemed a million miles away. The more I thought about home, the more I hated it. I hated the loneliness, the emptiness and the constant nagging. I hated the feeling of not being wanted, of being in the way, of being a nuisance. I could feel the tears welling up in my throat and suddenly the tears started to fall and I was sobbing.

"Florence, Florence, whatever is the matter my darling," said Aunty M rushing through the door and grabbing me in one of her huge bear hugs.

"Oh, Aunty M, I don't want to go home. I love it here so much. I am so sorry I upset you. I had no right. I will *never* forgive myself. I lied to you and went behind your back. Will you ever forgive me? Will you be able to forget?"

"Florence, please don't worry. I just think that your mum needs to speak to you. I just hope she will be able to pluck up the courage. I know we are all at fault and all to blame but it was all done for you, my darling. You are my very special girl, you know. Mum and dad will be here before you know it and then it will all become clear. At least I hope it will."

"So you forgive me Aunty M?"

"That goes without saying, my love."

Aunty M gave me a kiss on the forehead and wafted out of my room. I felt a little better. I got up to get a tissue from the dressing table and I looked out of the window at the night. I could hear the waves crashing on the beach below. I could smell the salt in the air. How was I going to leave all this behind for London's sirens, traffic and crowds?

I got back into bed and pulled the covers up right under my nose.

"Flo, Flo," came a whisper.

"Roma?" I whispered back.

Roma lay next to me in bed. She looked virtually transparent in her wispy white dress. Even her ginger curls looked pale, almost pink, and her skin a deathly white. If I had had any doubts about calling our grandparents, they disappeared and I knew I had no choice but to take the chance of upsetting everyone. I really didn't care. I knew what was most important.

"I'm glad you and Aunty M are friends again. What's happening on Saturday?"

"Well, all the family are coming on Saturday. Mum and Philip, granny and granpy so I'm going to call grandma and grandpa tomorrow and get them to come too. Then we will all be here and you can 'go' then. Ok?"

"Did you tell Aunty M you were going to invite them?" asked Roma.

"No, I didn't Roma. I don't want to give her the chance to say I can't. This is the last time I will have to go behind Aunty M's back. It has to be done though, doesn't it?"

Aunty Marmalade

"Flo, I am sorry for having to put all this on you but there was no one else."

"I know and I don't mind; you know I don't. I would do anything for you, Roma."

Roma smiled a watery smile.

Then together, we drifted off into a fitful sleep.

Chapter 32

Saturday morning dawned at last. Mum and Philip, granny and granpy were arriving at ten thirty. I had phoned my grandma and grandpa pretending that I was calling on behalf of the family to invite them for coffee and to meet everyone. They sounded a bit surprised at the invitation but agreed to come, saying that this was a wonderful opportunity to mend bridges. I sort of understood what they meant. Life was too short to bear grudges and an opportunity to say 'sorry' was overdue. They said they would arrive at eleven.

After breakfast, I packed my rucksack and Biggles and I had a last run on the beach together. It was a beautiful day. The sky was blue and the sea calm.

It was a perfect day for Roma to 'rest in peace.' As we

ran along, my tummy was churning. I was dreading

mum's reaction when she saw my grandparents. Of all

that was going to happen in the next two hours that was

what scared me most. I knew Aunty M would forgive

me. I knew my mum wouldn't. Well, she couldn't. She

wouldn't want to.

At ten thirty, I heard a car draw up. It was

granny and granpy. They hugged me and granny gave

me one of her lipsticky kisses on the cheek. Granpy

ruffled my curls and played pretend boxing just like he

always did. Five minutes later, another car drew up and

out got mum and Philip. They looked tanned and were

smiling.

So far so good. I walked outside to meet them.

There seemed no reason to hurry.

"Hello Florence," said my mum. "How are you?"

"I'm fine mum. How are you?" I lifted my arms up hoping she might do the same and give me a hug, but she didn't.

"We are fine too, thank you", she replied backing away from me. "Are you packed? Have you checked everywhere because we don't want to have to come all this way again to get what you've forgotten? I don't know why you couldn't come home by train."

"I would have if you had asked me, mum. I thought you wanted to come and collect me. Aunty M said so."

"Well, she would say that. Granny phoned and told us to come down. What have you been up to? I hope there's no trouble, Florence?" said mum and she stared at me with her piercing grey eyes that cut through me like a knife. I felt a sudden wave of

sickness hit me and I gulped.

"How's things, Florrie?"asked Philip smiling

and pulling my nose fondly just like he always did.

"Fine. Did you have a good time?" I asked him.

"Yes, it was good. I was busy but we did

manage to have a few days on the beach and we did

some sightseeing."

"That's good. Let's go in," I suggested. I

wanted us safely inside before my grandparents arrived.

"Best make sure you've got everything packed

and you've left nothing behind Florrie," said Philip

anxiously and giving me a wink. He didn't want

another upset either.

"I will. I'll check again, promise."

Together, we walked inside. Just as we closed

the front door, I heard a car pull up on the gravel drive.

My heart thumped in my chest and I knew there was no turning back now.

Chapter 33

"Did I hear a car?" said granny straining to look out of the sitting room window.

"I think you did," said Aunty M.

"Who could that be?" asked granpy.

I could feel my face getting hotter and imagined it turning beetroot red, "I'll go," I offered heading for the door.

I rushed out of the room and opened the front door. There standing on the doorstep were my grandparents smiling.

"Please come in," I said and I opened the door wide. I took a step back and trod on someone's toe. I swung around about to apologise to whoever it was. Standing there was Aunty M. She put out her hand and shook their hands vigorously. I looked at them and at Aunty M.

"I phoned Aunty M, Florence. Just to make sure. I hope you don't mind," said grandma.

"And I phoned granny so she was prepared," said Aunty M.

I could hardly believe my ears.

"What about mum?"

"We thought it best not to. We thought we would spring the surprise on her and then she could not back down. All this bad feeling and separation has gone on long enough and you are the most important person here, Florence," said Aunty M and with that she turned towards the sitting room. The three of us followed.

"What on earth is this?" asked my mum standing up. "What are they doing here?"

Aunty Marmalade

"We invited them, Helen. It is time all the secrets were out in the open after all this time. Florence found out about her father and her twin sister. We all need to forgive and forget. Time has moved on and we must all move on too," said Aunty M.

"What do you mean, we have to forgive and forget. I have nothing to forgive and forget. How dare you, Madeleine. You always were selfish. You always got your own way when we were growing up."

"No I didn't. Anyway, this is not the time for that. We have to think about Florence now. Her life has been turned upside down."

"What do you mean turned upside down?" spat my mum at her sister.

"Don't you realise the significance of all of this?" said Aunty M quietly.

"Yes I do," snarled my mum. "What you are saying is Florence needs to find out about her mother too. I think you should tell her, don't you. She obviously doesn't know that part, does she?"

"No she doesn't. Florence, there is something you should have been told and I could not pluck up the courage to tell you but now I know I must."

"What must you tell me, Aunty M? What haven't you told me?" I pleaded, dreading the answer.

"Madeleine, be careful," said granny getting up and grabbing me.

"What's going on? Please tell me," I pleaded again.

"Florence this was why they kept us apart," said grandma. "We knew you see."

"Why did they keep us apart? What's the big secret? Please tell me. It is not fair to do this to me," I said as the tears streamed down my face.

"Florence, the thing is," said Aunty M, "the thing is. I am your mum."

Chapter 34

I could not believe my ears. I stared at Aunty M.

I looked at my mum and Philip. I glared at granny and

granpy. I looked across at my father's parents. There

was silence. No-one said a word. You could cut the air

with a knife. I didn't know what to do. I had been

betrayed by everyone now. They all knew. They all

knew about Simon, Roma and my real mum. Everyone

knew everything and I had known nothing. Nothing at

all. How could they all treat me like this? I would

never, ever forgive any of them. They had kept secrets

from me. They lied to me. If you love someone, they

should never treat you in this way. I was even betrayed by Aunty M.

I wanted to run. I ran towards the door and shoved it open. I fled to the back door and ran across the lawn towards the cliff. Biggles, realising that a walk was on offer, ran out with me and together, we headed for the beach. I followed him down the steps to the sand and ran behind him. The salty sea air wisped round me and tears poured out of my eyes and my nose dripped.

I didn't care how I looked. I didn't care who saw me. I just had to get away from the lies and the secrets and the fact that I was unloved and unwanted. My father had died and I never got the chance to know him. Without realising it before, I was missing him. If only I had had the chance to talk to him just once. I ran out of breath and had to slow down. Yes, I thought as I dragged one foot after the other along the sand that is why mum disliked me so much. That was why she didn't want me. That was why I was nothing but a nuisance to her. The reasons for her behaviour towards me were; I *wasn't hers.*

But how had I ended up being brought up by her? She obviously didn't want me, did she? That had always been obvious to me even when I was really little. I could never remember her cuddling me or hugging me ever. I could never remember her saying how well I had done in my tests at school or my ballet exams. She had always just said, "And what did so-and-so get?" and if it was better than me, she smirked and walked off. So why did Aunty M give me away? *Omigod, omigod,* the thought suddenly struck me. *I needed to know.*

Aunty M had given me away to her sister.

But why?

Chapter 35

"Florence, come back," came a voice carried on the wind.

I spun around and saw Aunty M huffing and puffing down the beach towards me. I stopped realising it was foolish to keep going. I had to go back to find out what had happened.

"Florence, darling let's go back. We are all so worried about you. I didn't want you to find out this way. I had planned a better way but every time I tried to tell you I just couldn't pluck up the courage. I am so very sorry for what I have done to you. Let's go back and join the others."

Aunty Marmalade

Aunty M reached out her hand to me and smiled. Her rosy cheeks were wet with tears and her hair was bouncing around her face. She was out of breath and somehow she looked so desperate, so I smiled and took her hand. It was the first time I held the hand of my real mum.

We walked back to the cottage in silence. I didn't have anything to say. I was so choked up that I didn't think I could say anything even if I wanted to. We were still holding hands as we walked back into the sitting room. Granpy got up and ushered me to sit down in his place. He walked over to the piano stool and sat down.

"Well, Madeleine, I think our little Florence could do with a few explanations, don't you?" said granny.

"I think she needs some answers," said my grandma.

204

"I think we should leave them both in peace," said granny. "They have a lot to talk about. This has gone on far too long, too much hurt, too many secrets kept from our little granddaughter. Why on earth Helen did you let this happen like this? You selfish girl."

"What do you mean, you selfish girl? How dare you accuse me of being selfish? I brought her up even though she was not mine. I don't remember you all saying you would take her. I remember the excuses about you being too old and then Madeleine having that breakdown, going into the home and then running off to some Greek island and hiding away for five years. Yes Florence, that's what, happened. It was HER that wouldn't let Simon's parents see you so her secret wouldn't come out. She couldn't cope without Simon. Then Roma's death finished her off and she was incapable of looking after you so I stepped in and took you. I fed you and clothed you and did all I could for you. Philip didn't mind and we brought you up as our own even though I never wanted children of my own. Now this is the thanks I get. I have had enough of this. I am going home. I assume you will leave us now Florence and come and live with your real mum. I suppose, Madeleine, you want her or are you going to desert her again?"

"So you gave me away. How could you do that to me?" I said in disbelief.

"I was ill Florence. So much had happened to me. I couldn't cope. I couldn't look after you. Helen did not hesitate at the time to take you. Helen, I will always be in your debt. You saved me and Florence. Thank you."

"There was nothing else I could do, was there. I had no choice. But once you came home, you should have claimed her back. That was what you should have

206

done. Mum and dad gave you this cottage; you had

everything."

"Yes, why didn't you come to get me?" I asked

in desperation.

"You seemed so settled, with your school and

friends and everything. It seemed unkind to take you

back. I had no idea how to look after a five year old.

I'm not even sure whether I will be any good now,"

said Aunty M with desperation in her voice.

"But I'm sure you will know what to do. I will

help you and I'm no trouble, am I?" I stated.

"And I'm a hopeless mother anyway. I have my

career to think of. It has been hard for me to juggle

Florence and my job," said mum.

"I know I have been a nuisance," I said to my

mum. At last I had the answers to so many questions.

Now I knew that I had *not* been wrong. I had not been

wanted by the person I knew as my mum for all these years.

"Florence and I will stay together now. Isn't that right, Florence?"

And without hesitating I blurted out, "Yes it is, Mummy Marmalade."

With that granny and granpy, grandma and grandpa and Mummy Marmalade all grabbed me. Philip came up too and pulled my nose again. Even Helen smiled at me and I could tell she was relieved. Relieved to get rid of me and relieved to speak out at last after all these years. She and Mummy Marmalade said a few words which I couldn't hear and then one by one everyone left. There was talk of everyone making a date for Sunday lunch in two weeks time. Then they all left leaving Mummy M and me alone.

"I just can't believe you are my real mum. I never guessed. You and mum look so similar in those wedding photos. I just thought mum had married someone else and never told me. It never dawned on me that it was you in the photo. I didn't think you had ever married."

"Yes, I did. I married Simon. That is why when I told you about Roma and Simon, I kept saying 'mum' because that was me and you thought I meant Helen."

"Will I be able to move in Apple Jack's Cottage for good then?" I asked.

"This is your home, Florence. Helen is bringing down all your stuff from London when they all come from lunch in two weeks time."

"Mum?"

"Yes darling. Doesn't it sound funny, Flo. What is it?"

"I need to go to Roma's grave. I have to tell her all that has happened. Can I go now?"

"Of course. You can take some flowers. Do you want me to come?"

"No thank you. I would like to go on my own."

"That's fine, Flo. She needs to know about her mum, doesn't she?"

"Yes she does and I want to be the one to tell her," I said.

Chapter 36

I climbed up the stairs to the attic. Roma was sitting on the red sofa waiting for me like I guessed she would.

"Well we never guessed, did we?" said Roma.

"No we didn't, but at least now we know who our dad was and what happened to him. We know who our mum is. I just can't believe it though. I love Aunty M so much. She has made me feel so happy since I've been here. She treats me just like a grown up and now I won't have to go back to London. I don't know what will happen about school though. I may not be going to Saint Maur's now. But I don't care," I said with a big grin on my face. It was then I looked towards Roma. She was very faint now and her eyes were sad. I realised we had to get to her grave now before it was too late.

"Roma, come on we need to get you back to your grave."

"I know Flo, but I can't bear the thought of losing you."

"And I can't bear to lose you too. Is there any chance that you may be able to keep on visiting me?"

"I don't know. Once I have rested properly it may be that I won't be able to come back. But I heard someone say once, 'never say never' so if I can, I will. I will do anything to stay near to you."

"I'll go first then. Will you follow me?" I asked.

"I will," Roma replied.

I headed down the stairs and waved goodbye to Mummy M who was sitting in the kitchen drinking tea.

212

She smiled and waved back. Roma and I continued on our way. I stopped at the Post Office and bought a bunch of freesias because of their lovely smell and also because Roma pointed to them as her favourites.

We arrived at the grave. I pulled out the old flowers and put the freesias in their place. Roma floated over to the grave and lay down.

"Thank you, Flo for bringing everyone together and bringing out all their secrets. Now everyone is talking and you can all carry on with the rest of your lives. I just wish I could be part of it all with you. I'll find dad and have a word with him when I get over to the other side, and see if there is any way I can come back. I'll send you a sign. He may be able to visit you too. Never say never."

"What will the sign be?"

"Don't know. But you'll guess, I'm sure."

Aunty Marmalade

Out of nowhere, the wind blew. It howled around me making my curls fly and tangle into millions of knots. I grabbed my hair, dreading the telling off I would get from mum. Then I remembered that that would never happen again. Mummy M understood how easily hair can get into knots. She wouldn't mind. She would help me untangle the knots I knew she would. My life was going to change now. I sighed with a smile. I had so much to look forward to now.

As I looked towards the grave, Roma had gone. An emptiness overwhelmed me and I fought back the tears. The wind quietened down and suddenly I felt very alone. I turned around and started to walk back home. Home. It sounded good. I walked back home to my real mum and my new future.

For years Ruth Young has been teaching children and young adults but her passion has always been storytelling. She is currently working on a sequel to Aunty Marmalade and is in the process of publishing another book for young readers. Mrs. Young and her husband, an airline pilot, have two daughters studying at University. She loves to travel and enjoys writing her stories wherever she goes. Mrs. Young and her husband live in Surrey, England.

Lightning Source UK Ltd.
Milton Keynes UK
17 December 2009

147661UK00001B/68/P